Grace
Miller

THE
FOURTEENTH
GOLDFISH

Also by Jennifer L. Holm

The Babymouse series (with Matthew Holm)
The Squish series (with Matthew Holm)
Boston Jane: An Adventure
Boston Jane: Wilderness Days
Boston Jane: The Claim
The Creek
Middle School Is Worse Than Meatloaf
Eighth Grade Is Making Me Sick
Our Only May Amelia
The Trouble with May Amelia
Penny from Heaven
Turtle in Paradise
The Stink Files series (with Jonathan Hamel)

THE FOURTEENTH GOLDFISH

JENNIFER L. HOLM

Random House New York

Text copyright © 2014 by Jennifer L. Holm
Jacket art and interior illustrations copyright © 2014 by Tad Carpenter

Visit us on the Web! randomhouse.com/kids

Educators and librarians, for a variety of teaching tools, visit us at
RHTeachersLibrarians.com

Library of Congress Cataloging-in-Publication Data
Holm, Jennifer L., author.
The fourteenth goldfish / Jennifer L. Holm. — First edition.
p. cm
Summary: Ellie's scientist grandfather has discovered a way to reverse aging, and consequently has turned into a teenager—which makes for complicated relationships when he moves in with Ellie and her mother, his daughter.
ISBN 978-0-375-87064-4 (trade) — ISBN 978-0-375-97064-1 (lib. bdg.) —
ISBN 978-0-307-97436-5 (ebook)
1. Grandfathers—Juvenile fiction. 2. Scientists—Juvenile fiction. 3. Aging—Juvenile fiction. 4. Families—Juvenile fiction. [1. Grandfathers—Fiction. 2. Scientists—Fiction. 3. Aging—Fiction. 4. Family life—Fiction.] I. Title.
PZ7.H732226Fo 2014
813.6—dc23 2013035052

Printed in the United States of America
10 9 8 7 6 5 4
First Edition

For Jonathan, Will & Millie—my mad scientists

Contents

You cannot teach a man anything;
you can only help him discover it in himself.
—Galileo Galilei

THE FOURTEENTH GOLDFISH

1
Goldie

When I was in preschool, I had a teacher named Starlily. She wore rainbow tie-dyed dresses and was always bringing in cookies that were made with granola and flax and had no taste.

Starlily taught us to sit still at snack time, sneeze into our elbows, and not eat the Play-Doh (which most kids seemed to think was optional). Then one day, she sent all of us home with a goldfish. She got

I

them at ten for a dollar at a pet store. She gave our parents a lecture before sending us off.

"The goldfish will teach your child about the cycle of life." She explained, "Goldfish don't last very long."

I took my goldfish home and named it Goldie like every other kid in the world who thought they were being original. But it turned out that Goldie *was* kind of original.

Because Goldie didn't die.

Even after all my classmates' fish had gone to the great fishbowl in the sky, Goldie was still alive. Still alive when I started kindergarten. Still alive in first grade. Still alive in second grade and third and fourth. Then finally, last year in fifth grade, I went into the kitchen one morning and saw my fish floating upside down in the bowl.

My mom groaned when I told her.

"He didn't last very long," she said.

"What are you talking about?" I asked. "He lasted seven years!"

She gave me a smile and said, "Ellie, that wasn't

the original Goldie. The first fish only lasted two weeks. When he died, I bought another one and put him in the bowl. There've been a *lot* of fish over the years."

"What number was this one?"

"Unlucky thirteen," she said with a wry look.

"They were all unlucky," I pointed out.

We gave Goldie Thirteen a toilet-bowl funeral, and I asked my mom if we could get a dog.

2
Puzzles

We live in a house that looks like a shoe box. It has two bedrooms and a bathroom, which has a toilet that's always getting clogged. I secretly think it's haunted by all the fish that were flushed down it.

Our backyard is tiny—just a slab of concrete that barely fits a table and chairs. It's the reason my mom won't let me get a dog. She says it wouldn't be fair, that a dog needs a real yard to run around in.

My babysitter Nicole walks into the kitchen, where I'm putting together a puzzle. It's kind of taken over our table.

"You've been working on that forever, Ellie," she says. "How many pieces is it?"

"One thousand," I say.

It's a picture of New York City—a street scene with yellow cabs. I love puzzles. I like trying to figure out how things fit together. How a curve meets a curve and the perfect angle of a corner piece.

"I'm going to be on Broadway someday," she tells me.

Nicole has long buttery hair and looks like she should be in a shampoo commercial. She played Juliet in the production of *Romeo and Juliet* that my mother directed at the local high school. My mom's a high school drama teacher and my dad's an actor. They got divorced when I was little, but they're still friends.

They're always telling me I need to find my passion. Specifically, they'd like me to be passionate about theater. But I'm not. Sometimes I wonder if

I was born into the wrong family. Being onstage makes me nervous (I've watched too many actors flub their lines), and I'm not a fan of working behind the scenes, either (I always end up steaming costumes).

"Oh, yeah. Your mom called. She's gonna be late," Nicole says. Almost as an afterthought, she adds, "Something to do with getting your grandfather from the police."

For a second, I think I heard wrong.

"What?" I ask. "Is he okay?"

She lifts her shoulders. "She didn't say. But she said we can order a pizza."

An hour later, my belly is full of pizza, but I'm still confused.

"Did my mom say anything about why Grandpa was with the police?" I ask.

Nicole looks mystified. "No. Does he get in trouble a lot?"

I shake my head. "I don't think so. I mean, he's old," I say.

"How old is he?"

I'm not quite sure. I've never really thought about it, actually. He's always just looked "old" to me: wrinkled, gray-haired, holding a cane. Your basic grandparent.

We only see him two or three times a year, usually at a Chinese restaurant. He always orders moo goo gai pan and steals packets of soy sauce to take home. I often wonder what he does with them. He doesn't live that far from us, but he and my mother don't get along very well. He's a scientist and says theater isn't a real job. He's still mad that she didn't go to Harvard like he did.

A car alarm goes off in the distance.

"Maybe he was in a car accident?" Nicole suggests. "I don't know why teenagers get a bad rap, because old people are way worse drivers."

"He doesn't drive anymore."

"Maybe he wandered off." Nicole taps her head. "My neighbor had Alzheimer's. She got out all the time. The police always brought her home."

It kind of sounds like she's describing a dog.

"That's so sad," I say.

Nicole nods. "Totally sad. The last time she ran away, she got hit by a car! How crazy is that?"

I stare at her with my mouth open.

"But I'm sure *your* grandfather's fine," she says.

Then she flips back her hair and smiles. "Hey! Want to make some popcorn and watch a movie?"

3
Ring

Warm air drifts through my bedroom window. We live in the Bay Area, in the shadow of San Francisco, and late-September nights can be cool. But it's hot tonight, like summer is refusing to leave.

I used to love how my bedroom was decorated, but lately I'm not so sure. The walls are covered with the painted handprints of me and my best friend, Brianna. We started doing them back in first grade and added more handprints every year. You can

9

see my little handprints grow bigger, like a time capsule of my life.

But we haven't done any yet this school year, or even this summer, because Brianna found her passion: volleyball. She's busy every second now with clinics and practices and weekend tournaments. The truth is, I'm not even sure if she's still my best friend.

It's late when the garage door finally grinds open. I hear my mother talking to Nicole in the front hall, and I go to them.

"Thanks for staying," she tells Nicole.

My mom looks frazzled. Her mascara is smudged beneath her eyes, her red lipstick chewed away. Her natural hair color is dirty blond like mine, but she colors it. Right now, it's purple.

"No problem," Nicole replies. "Is your dad okay?"

An unreadable expression crosses my mom's face. "Oh, he's fine. Thanks for asking. Do you need a ride home?"

"I'm good!" Nicole says. "By the way, Lissa, I have some exciting news!"

"Yes?"

"I got a job at the mall! Isn't that great?"

"I didn't know you were looking," my mom says, confused.

"Yeah, I didn't think I'd get it. It's such a big opportunity. The ear-piercing place at the mall!"

"When do you start?" my mom asks.

"That's the hard part. They want me to start tomorrow afternoon. So I can't watch Ellie anymore. I totally would have given you more notice, but . . ."

"I understand," my mom says, and I can hear the strain in her voice.

Nicole turns to me. "I forgot to tell you. I get a discount! Isn't that great? So come by anytime and shop."

"Uh, okay," I say.

"I better be going," she says. "Good night!"

"Good night," my mother echoes.

I stand in the doorway with my mother and watch her walk out into the night.

"Did she just quit?" I ask. I'm a little in shock.

My mother nods. "This is turning into a banner day."

I stare out into the night to catch a last glimpse of my babysitter, but see someone else: a boy with long hair. He's standing beneath the old, dying palm tree on our front lawn. It drops big brown fronds everywhere, and my mom says it needs to come down.

The boy is slender, wiry-looking. He looks thirteen, maybe fourteen? It's hard to tell with boys sometimes.

"You need to put your trash out," the boy calls to my mom. Tomorrow is trash day and our neighbors' trash cans line the street.

"Would you please come inside already?" my mom tells the boy.

"And when's the last time you fertilized the lawn?" he asks. "There's crabgrass."

"It's late," my mom says, holding the door open impatiently.

I wonder if he's one of my mom's students. Sometimes they help her haul stuff in and out of her big, battered cargo van.

"You have to maintain your house if you want it to maintain its value," he says.

"Now!"

The boy reluctantly picks up a large duffel bag and walks into our house.

He doesn't look like the typical theater-crew kid. They usually wear jeans and T-shirts, stuff that's easy to work in. This kid's wearing a rumpled pin-stripe shirt, khaki polyester pants, a tweed jacket with patches on the elbows, and leather loafers. But it's his socks that stand out the most: they're black dress socks. You don't see boys in middle school wearing those a lot. It's like he's on his way to a bar mitzvah.

He stares at me with piercing eyes.

"Did you make honor roll?"

I'm startled, but answer anyway.

"Uh, we haven't gotten report cards yet."

Something about the boy seems familiar. His hair is dark brown, on the shaggy side, and the ends are dyed gray. An actor from one of my mom's shows, maybe?

"Who are you?" I ask him.

He ignores me.

"You need good grades if you're going to get into a competitive PhD program."

"PhD program? She's eleven years old!" my mother says.

"You can't start too early. Speaking of which," he says, looking pointedly at my mother's outfit, "is *that* what you wear to work?"

My mom likes to raid the theater wardrobe closet at school. This morning, she left the house in a floor-length black satin skirt and matching bolero jacket with a frilly white poet's shirt.

"Maybe you should consider buying a nice pant-suit," he suggests.

"Still stuck in the Stone Age, I see," she shoots back.

Then he turns and looks at me, taking in my tank-top-and-boxer-shorts pajama set.

He says, "Why are your pajamas so short? Whatever happened to long nightgowns? Are you boy-crazy like your mother was?"

"All the girls her age wear pajamas like that," my mom answers for me. "And I wasn't boy-crazy!"

"You must've been boy-crazy to elope," he says.

"I was in love," she says through gritted teeth.

"A PhD lasts a lot longer than love," he replies. "It's not too late to go back to school. You could still get a real degree."

Something about this whole exchange tickles at my memory. It's like watching a movie I've already seen. I study the boy—the gray-tipped hair, the way he's standing so comfortably in our hall, how his right hand opens and closes as if used to grasping something by habit. But it's the heavy gold ring hanging loosely on his middle finger that draws my eye. It's a school ring, like the kind you get in college, and it looks old and worn and has a red gem in the center.

"I've seen that ring before," I say, and then I remember whose hand I saw it on.

I look at the boy.

"Grandpa?" I blurt out.

4
Magician

"Who were you expecting?" he asks. "The tooth fairy?"

He seems like a thirteen-year-old boy, but when I look really closely I can see hints of my grandfather. The watery blue eyes. The slightly snarky set of his mouth. The way his eyebrows meet in the middle.

"Is this some kind of magic?" I ask.

The boy curls his lips and looks at my mother. "You're raising *my* granddaughter to believe in magic? This is what happens when you major in drama." He says "drama" like it's a bad word.

"Whatever, Dad," my mom says, sounding like a bored teenager.

"This is science, plain and simple," he says to me.

But I don't see anything simple about it and just shake my head.

He gives an exasperated sigh. "It should be perfectly obvious. I engineered a way to reverse senescence through cellular regeneration."

I stare at him.

"In layman's terms: I discovered a cure for aging." His voice shakes with excitement. "In effect, I have discovered the fountain of youth!"

I don't know what to believe. On the one hand, he sounds just like my grandfather. I'm half-tempted to see if he has any soy sauce in the pockets of his jacket. On the other hand, I'm not totally sure I believe any of it. Part of me wonders if this is just some weirdo who stole my grandfather's ring and is tricking my mom. She's a sucker for kids with sad stories.

I turn to her. "Are you sure it's Grandpa?"

She rolls her eyes. "It's him, all right."

"Of course it's me!" the boy says indignantly. He whips out an old man's worn leather wallet and shows me his driver's license. My grandfather's cranky face stares back from the photo, and the look in his eyes is exactly the same as on the boy's face.

"This is so cool," I whisper.

"Cool? It's historic! They're going to give me a Nobel!" His voice gets louder. "Melvin Herbert Sagarsky will be a household name!"

My mom yawns. She's clearly unimpressed. Or maybe just tired. It's pretty late.

"I'm going to bed. Why don't you bond with *your* granddaughter?" She gives my grandfather a look. "And don't put anything strange in the refrigerator."

My mom tells stories of how when she was little, my grandfather would keep experiments in the refrigerator. There would be stacks of petri dishes next to the cottage cheese and butter.

Then we're alone in the kitchen. My grandfather's stomach growls loudly.

"Got anything to eat in this place?" he demands. "I'm starving."

"There's pizza," I tell him.

He stands at the counter and wolfs down the rest of the pizza.

"The lab assistants live on this stuff when they run experiments at night," he says.

Then he goes to the fridge, takes out the milk, and pours himself a big glass. He drinks it and pours himself another.

He waves the carton of milk at me and burps. "Make sure you take your calcium. Everything they say about bone density is true. I lost two inches in the last ten years of my life."

"You shrank?"

"The perils of old age," he says.

"At least you got your hair back now," I point out.

"I got back more than my hair!" His eyes glitter. "My eyes are twenty-twenty, my hearing is perfect, and my arthritis is gone!" He wiggles his fingers.

"What did you get picked up by the police for?" I ask.

"They said I was trespassing on private property," he says. "I got let off with a warning."

"Where?"

"My laboratory!" His voice trembles with outrage. "I practically built that place! I have credits on nineteen of their patents, you know. You'd think they'd have some respect."

I nod even though I have no idea what a patent is.

"Ever since the company brought in those fast-talking investors, everything's been different. It's all maximizing-profits this and minimizing-risks that. They have no respect for science."

Then he yawns. The energy seems to go out of

him in a rush, like a switch flicked off, and his shoulders slump. The illusion fades, and all at once he looks like any other tired thirteen-year-old boy who needs a haircut.

"Where am I sleeping?" he asks.

5
Jellyfish

I'm always the first one up in the morning because I like to cook breakfast. My mom hates cooking and jokes that she doesn't know if I'm really her kid. But I feel comfortable in the kitchen. There's an order to it, and it's fun to experiment.

Lately, I've been making what I call Crazy-Mixed-Up Pancakes. I use a basic pancake batter and add different ingredients. So far, I've made a s'mores version (chocolate, marshmallows, graham

22

cracker crumbles), a banana split version (bananas, chocolate bits, maraschino cherry), and a piña colada one (pineapples, coconut).

This morning, I make an old standby—peanut butter cup. I use peanut butter morsels and chocolate chips. I'm just plating up the pancakes when my grandfather walks into the kitchen. He's wearing old-man pajamas, the button-up cotton kind, and his hair is tied back with one of my ponytail holders. He must have found it in the bathroom.

"Something's wrong with the toilet," he tells me. "I had to use the plunger."

"That happens a lot. Want some pancakes?" I ask him.

"Thanks," he says, and takes a plate.

He eats fast and then helps himself to seconds. Teenage boys really eat a lot, I guess.

He's got a bad case of bed head, something I'm all too familiar with; my hair's the exact same way. It's frizzy and flyaway and I've always hated it. I wonder if I got it from him.

"I have a good spray that works on frizzies," I tell him.

He waves his spoon at me. "I have more important things to worry about than hair. I need to get my *T. melvinus* out of the lab. It's what helped me sort out the mechanism for reversing senescence."

"What's senescence?" It sounds like a terrible disease.

"Senescence is the process of aging."

I was kind of right. "So what's *T. melvinus*?"

"It stands for *Turritopsis melvinus*. It's a species of jellyfish."

"A jellyfish did this to you? Are you kidding me?"

He lifts an eyebrow. "Why is it so hard to believe? There have always been examples of regenerative abilities in nature."

"There have?"

My grandfather leans forward, his face intent. "Take the planarian flatworm. You can slice it in two and each part will grow into a new worm. The hydra, a freshwater creature, can actually regenerate body parts, and the sea anemone doesn't appear to experience senescence *at all.*"

I have never heard about any of this before.

"Then there's *Turritopsis nutricula.*" His voice is full of wonder. "*T. nutricula* is a jellyfish that can actually revert its body to the polyp stage. *To its younger self!*"

This is so interesting. *He's* so interesting. It's like I've never really listened to him before. And maybe I haven't. Usually when we're together, he and my mom just bicker.

"How do you know so much about this?" I ask.

"Because I've been researching it for the last forty years. It's my side project. I've had articles published, you know."

I'm starting to think that maybe I don't know him at all. Not really. It's like he's been playing the part of Grandfather in a play, but underneath the makeup is something more. A real person.

"A few months ago, an Australian diver in the Philippines contacted me because he read on the Internet that I was researching jellyfish. He thought he'd found an odd specimen of *T. nutricula*. I asked him to ship it to me. The typical *T. nutricula* is small, a few millimeters. The size of the nail on your pinkie finger." He holds out his pinkie finger. "But the *T. nutricula* specimen he sent me was huge, more than three hundred millimeters."

"I always get confused about the millimeter-to-inches thing," I admit.

"It was a foot in diameter," he explains. "And there were other anomalies. I knew it was a new species. I even named it: *Turritopsis melvinus*."

"Shouldn't it have been named after the guy who found it?" I ask.

He scoffs. "All he did was catch it. I *identified* it. I was the one who did all the work. I was the one who created the compound. I was the one who tested it on the mice."

"You experimented on mice?" That seems way worse than flushing goldfish down the toilet.

"Adult mice," he says. "A few days after I injected them with the compound, they reverted to an adolescent stage."

"They became teenagers?" I try to picture mice with pimples and long hair.

"Exactly!" he exclaims. "So I injected it in myself and the rest is history! I was trying to get the rest of the *T. melvinus* specimen out of the lab when the rent-a-cop busted me."

I think for a moment.

"Couldn't you just call up your old bosses and tell them what happened? I mean, this is kind of a big breakthrough, right? I bet they'd be pretty excited."

"They don't even know it's there." His gaze hardens. "Besides, they'll just take all the credit. This is *my* discovery."

"Good morning, campers!" my mom trills.

Today she's wearing one of her standard outfits— a neon-purple dress that hits her above the knees and high black boots.

My grandfather gasps when he sees her.

"Melissa! You can't go to work in that!"

"What's wrong with it?" my mother asks.

"I can see the top of your thighs!"

She waves off his concern and starts gathering her bags. "Let's get moving or we're going to be late."

"Late for what?" he asks.

"School, of course."

"School?" he sputters. "I already went to school. I have two PhDs, in case you've forgotten."

"Too bad. You're going. I called Bernadette this morning." Bernadette is the middle school secretary and one of my mother's friends.

"What did you tell her?" I ask.

She tips her head at my grandfather. "That *Melvin* here is my distant cousin's kid. His dad died and his mom remarried a meth addict. He doesn't get along with the new stepfather, who he secretly suspects started the fire that burned down the trailer with his dad in it. So he hitchhiked up here and I took him in."

"That's really good," I tell her.

"Your dad will be pleased to hear it," she said. "It's from a play he wrote in college—*Hamlet in Fresno*. I directed it."

My grandfather interrupts us.

"Why can't I just stay here? I am perfectly capable of looking after myself!" He sounds like every other teenager in the world.

"Did you forget that the police released you into my custody? I work with kids. I'm a teacher. I can't have a thirteen-year-old truant in my house. Someone will see you and I'll lose my job."

There's a beat of silence as he stares at the floor.

"Fine. I'll go," he mutters.

"Great." Then she adds, "By the way, you're Ellie's new babysitter."

6

Crispy Corn Dog

At the end of fifth grade, there was a formal graduation ceremony. Everyone got dressed up, and parents came and took pictures. We even got a diploma with a ribbon around it.

Afterward, my dad, my mom, her boyfriend, Ben, and I went out for dinner at my favorite Mexican place, a hole-in-the-wall where they give free refills of chips.

"No offense, Ellie," Ben said while we waited for

our food. "I think it's a little ridiculous to have a graduation for elementary school."

Ben doesn't say much, but when he opens his mouth, it's always interesting.

"I think it's nice to celebrate their achievement," my mother said.

Ben chuckled. "Getting through elementary school is hardly an achievement. Now, middle school? That's a different story."

My father grimaced. "They should give you a medal for surviving that."

At the time, I didn't understand what he meant. But I do now. Middle school is like one of those highway restrooms in the middle of nowhere. It's dirty and smelly, and it's crowded with strange people. By the time I graduated from elementary school, I knew everyone. I had watched them grow up and they had watched me. We knew who'd wet their pants in kindergarten, and whose father always screamed too loud at the coach during T-ball games. We had no secrets, and it was comfortable. But in middle school there are so many new kids. Some seem like they're from different planets.

Like the goth kid. He's always in black—pants, T-shirt, thick jacket, heavy Doc Martens. He has a pierced ear, eyebrow, and nose; he must set off metal detectors in the airport. Then there are the two girls who dress like twins even though they're clearly not. They wear the exact same outfits, down to the same socks. I've heard them talk in the halls and they finish each other's sentences.

I go through the hot-lunch line and look around for where to sit in the lunch court. We don't have a cafeteria; we eat outside with seagulls hovering overhead. They've been known to swoop down and grab fries off trays.

The girl who's my lab partner in science has an open seat next to her. Her name's Momo and she went to a different elementary school from me. But then I see Brianna; she's with a bunch of girls from the volleyball team. The seat across from her is free, so I slide in with my bought lunch—crispy corn dog and potato wedges with orange slices.

"You cut your hair?" I say, surprised.

Brianna's hair has always been long like mine. We got bangs at the same time, third grade. We even pool our money so we can buy cool ponytail holders with glittery bows and neon feathers and rainbow ribbons to share.

But she won't need those now. Her hair's been chopped short, in a sharp angled bob. I'd never be able to pull off that sleek haircut—my hair's way too crazy.

"It's easier for volleyball," she explains.

She looks pretty, but she doesn't look like Brianna.

I point to my lunch.

"Look! A crispy corn dog!" I tell her.

She snickers.

It's an inside joke. We both love corn dogs. We even made up a commercial featuring the crispy corn dog.

I say my part, "You can do anything with a crispy corn dog. It slices. It dices."

Brianna chimes in, "The crispy corn dog can fold up into a blanket. You can nap on it!"

We get more and more ridiculous.

"It writes book reports!"

"It makes dogs meow!"

We laugh, and it almost feels like old times.

I hold out my crispy corn dog.

"You want half?"

She hesitates and then gives a little shake of her bobbed head. "Coach is really on our case to eat healthy."

"Do you want to sleep over Saturday night?" I ask her.

She looks uncomfortable. "Tournament."

"Right," I say.

I remember the time I went fishing at summer camp. I didn't catch anything, no matter how many times I threw my line with the worm in the water.

I listen as they talk volleyball. They think the coach is tough, some girl named Serena needs to work on her serve, the hotel they are staying at this weekend has a pool.

One of the girls stands abruptly with her tray and says, "We don't want to be late."

"Late for what?" I ask Brianna.

"There's a team meeting about our fund-raiser," she explains. "Bake sale."

"Bye," I say, but she's already gone.

I stare at my corn dog and wonder if I'm the stupid worm.

A tray smacks down on the table across from me.

"Can you believe this?" my grandfather demands.

He's wearing navy-blue polyester pants, a button-up shirt with a tie, and a V-neck sweater with his tweed jacket. He definitely stands out fashion-wise.

"Three dollars for school lunch?" he says. "This is a bargain!"

He polishes his corn dog off in a few bites and then looks at my untouched lunch.

"Are you going to eat that?" he asks.

"Crispy corn dog: it makes you young again," I joke.

"What are you talking about?"

I sigh and push it over.

7

Our Town

The public bus after school is crowded, and some-one's been eating too much garlic. My grand-father has been complaining the whole way home.

He's not a fan of middle school. He says it's bor-ing and a waste of time, especially gym. But it's the textbooks that have him really riled up. He waves his science book at me.

"Can you believe it? Not a word! Not a footnote! Totally glossed over!"

"What?" I ask.

"Me! *I* should be in this book!"

The bus stops and kids shuffle off.

My grandfather stares at the textbook. "How can they not mention Sagarsky?"

"Probably because Sagarsky is a quack," a voice behind us says.

We turn around. It's the goth kid. He only takes the bus once in a while; he usually gets a ride from an older kid in a beat-up car.

"A quack? A quack?" my grandfather sputters. "Who are you?"

The kid introduces himself. "Raj." He looks at me, a long tuft of black hair flopping over his forehead.

"I'm Ellie. Ellie Cruz. And this is my gra—" I start to say, and stop myself. "My cousin. Melvin."

My grandfather glares at Raj. "What do you have against Sagarsky, anyway?"

"My science teacher says it's quacks like Sagarsky that give real scientists a bad name."

"*Bad name?* Sagarsky's a respected scientist!" my grandfather protests.

Raj shrugs. "Well, my teacher says he's just another in a line of charlatans looking for the fountain of youth."

The bus brakes squeal.

"This is our stop," I tell my grandfather, pulling him after me. I look at Raj. "Nice to meet you."

He nods. "See you around."

My grandfather glowers at him as he passes.

"Not if I have any say in the matter!"

"I cast my leads!" my mother announces when she walks into the kitchen. "Let's order takeout to celebrate!"

She goes to the drawer where we keep menus and starts riffling through them.

"How about Thai? Or Burmese?" she suggests. "Or there's a new Korean barbecue place I've been dying to check out."

"I don't eat any of that stuff," my grandfather says.

"If you tried it, you might like it," she cajoles him.

A belligerent look crosses his face. "I don't want to try it. I like Chinese food. It's reliable. You can walk into any Chinese restaurant and know what you're getting."

All this talk of Chinese food has made me hungry.

"I'll take a wonton soup," I say.

My mother sighs.

"Fine," she says, and a little of the excitement goes out of her voice.

When my mom returns from picking up the food, we settle in on stools at the counter. My grandfather digs around in his carton suspiciously.

"This doesn't look like the moo goo gai pan I usually get. This looks spicy. You know I don't like spicy food, Melissa."

"It's regular old moo goo gai pan, Dad," my mom says.

My grandfather takes a bite. Delivers the verdict.

"It's not spicy," he says.

"Good," my mother replies. "I was really worried."

"Humph," he says. "Did you ask for extra soy sauce?"

"Yes, Dad. It's in the bag," she says, rolling her eyes at me. "Well, in other news, the kids I cast as Emily and George are amazing!"

My grandfather's head snaps up. "You're doing *Our Town*? That show is a snooze."

He's right; I've seen it before and not much happens. It's basically just about these people who live in a small town called Grover's Corners. My mom likes to stage it because it has a big cast, so lots of kids can get a part.

My mom starts lecturing him like he's one of her students. "Excuse me, but *Our Town* is quite possibly the best play ever written about the totality of the human experience."

"Too bad it's so boring," my grandfather snarks.

"You have no idea what you're talking about. It's an amazing play. A hallmark of American playwriting. You just don't have any flair for drama."

40

My grandfather yawns widely.

The phone rings and I leap up to answer it.

"Bonjour," my dad says in a hearty voice.

I take the phone into the hallway.

"Hey, Dad! How's it going?"

"I'm tired of chasing Jean Valjean every night. But I'm not going to complain."

He got the part of Javert in a touring production of *Les Misérables*. He's been on the road since August. The play is a big break for him, but it doesn't feel the same without him around. My dad's the one who stayed home with me when I was little so that my mom could get her teaching degree. He says trying to keep a toddler entertained was the best acting experience he's ever had.

"Where are you?" I ask.

"Iowa City."

"Do they have a pool in the hotel?"

"Yep. Indoor."

"The toilet's been getting clogged up again," I tell him.

My father groans. "I'll take a look at it when I

swing back through." Even though he doesn't live here, he always takes care of house things for my mom.

"I miss you," I say.

"I miss you, too," he says.

My grandfather says something loudly and my mother shouts back. Their voices carry into the hall.

"Sounds like there's company," my dad says.

"Grandpa's over for dinner."

"Don't tell me: you're having Chinese," he says in a dry voice.

"How did you know?"

My father snorts over the phone. "That old man never changes."

I look back at my grandfather in the kitchen. He's slumped in the chair, his long hair brushing his shoulders, his shirt hanging on his skinny body.

"I don't know about that," I say.

8

The Possible

I have science first period. My teacher's name is Mr. Ham, and all the kids make fun of him behind his back by doing oinking sounds. But I kind of like him. He's funny and wears silly ties that have lobsters and cupcakes.

I barely made it to class in time this morning because we were running late. My grandfather wouldn't leave until he finished printing out something from the Internet. I didn't even have time to go to my locker and get my science textbook.

Naturally, the first thing Mr. Ham says is "Please open your textbooks to page thirty."

I groan.

"You can share with me," Momo whispers, and slides her book between us.

"Thanks," I whisper back.

At lunch, it's sloppy joe day. No one's exactly sure what's in the sloppy joes, but everyone agrees that they're gross.

After I get through the lunch line, I'm looking for Brianna when I hear someone shouting my name.

"Ellie! Over here!" My grandfather is sitting at a table and waving wildly at me. "I saved you a seat."

He's wearing another interesting outfit today: white button-up shirt with a light blue tie, polyester khakis, and, of course, black dress socks. The quirkiest part of his outfit is the ponytail holder.

It's one of mine—a bright pink one—and it kind of works on him.

He taps a pile of papers in front of him.

"I'm going to show that Raj character!"

That's what he's been calling him—"that Raj character."

"Is that what you were printing out this morning?" I ask. "What are they, anyway?"

"My articles."

"Articles?"

"I told you I've published quite a lot. I'm very well known. I have a virtual fan club in Finland, you know," he says.

"You're famous?"

His shoulders dip a little.

"It only has two hundred and thirty-one members," he admits. "But even so, they're going to go nuts when I finally announce my success with *T. melvinus.* I'm going to be the next Jonas Salk!"

It's like he's talking about a relative who I'm supposed to know but have never met.

"Who's Jonas Salk?" I ask.

My grandfather shakes his head. "Are you learning anything at all in this place?" He looks past me. "If this country spent half as much time on science education as cheering some idiot with a ball, you'd know who Jonas Salk is."

I turn to see what he's looking at and feel a stab of pain. At the edge of the lunch court, a bunch of girls are throwing a volleyball around. Brianna's with them. She spikes the ball and the girls collapse on the ground in laughter. I force myself to look away.

"Tell me about Salk," I say.

"Jonas Salk developed the vaccine for polio."

I'm almost afraid to ask, but I do anyway. "What's polio?"

"Polio is a terrible disease! It left children crippled. Killed them. Salk and his group of scientists pioneered a vaccine to prevent it. He even tested it on himself."

"Himself?" This seems nuts to me, like Dr. Jekyll and Mr. Hyde. "Was he a mad scientist or something?"

46

My grandfather sits up straighter, stares at me hard.

"All scientists are a little bit mad, Ellie."

For a moment, I think he's kidding, but then I realize he's serious.

"Average people just give up at the obstacles we face every day. Scientists fail again and again and again. Sometimes for our whole lives. But we don't give up, because we want to solve the puzzle."

"I like puzzles," I say.

"Yes, but have you ever tried to put a puzzle together and given up because it was too hard?"

I nod.

"Scientists *never* give up. They keep trying because they believe in the possible."

"The possible?"

"That it's *possible* to create a cure for polio. That it's *possible* to sequence the human genome. That it's *possible* to find a way to reverse aging. That science can change the world."

And I get it.

A palm tree sways in the breeze, its fronds brown and shedding. Something shifts inside me, like a puzzle piece snapping into place.

I look at my grandfather. "I think I know where Raj hangs out after school."

9
Fruit

aj is waiting at the curb. His eyes are fixed on the cars driving up and down the street.

My grandfather stomps over to him, digging in his backpack. It's my old one from elementary school; it has kittens on it. I thought it was a little uncool for him, but he told me it was a perfectly good backpack and he didn't care what people might think.

"You!" my grandfather shouts.

Raj turns, watches us. His eyes flicker to me briefly before returning to my grandfather.

My grandfather pulls out the papers and shoves them into Raj's hands.

"Read 'em and weep," he says.

Raj scans them. Then he looks up.

"Most of these were published over thirty years ago."

My grandfather is stunned into a momentary silence, then says, "Einstein published a long time ago, too. Are you gonna pooh-pooh him?"

"You're being a little ridiculous," Raj says.

A compact car pulls up to the curb, a teenager behind the wheel. He has the same dark eyes as Raj but looks a few years older. Raj folds his tall frame into the front seat.

"Ridiculous, huh?" my grandfather sputters. "What do you know, anyway? You're just a kid."

Raj leans out the open window, gives my grandfather a slow look.

"I don't know. You're a kid, too." He pauses. "What do *you* know?"

O O O

When we get home, my grandfather heads straight for the kitchen.

"I'm starving," he says.

"I'll heat up some burritos," I say. There's probably not a more perfect combination than rice, refried beans, and cheese.

He makes himself a cup of hot tea to go with his burrito. He pours the steaming water into the mug with precision, adds two perfect spoonfuls of sugar, and methodically stirs the sugar like he's making a formula. It makes me think of the mad scientist conversation.

"I liked what you talked about at lunch," I confess. "About science. But how do you start?"

He looks up from his tea. "What do you mean?"

"In a puzzle, I always begin with a straight-edge piece. If you wanted to cure polio or anything, where would you even start?"

"With your eyes, of course," he says.

"Eyes?"

51

He looks at the bowl of fruit on the counter.

"For example, that bowl of fruit. What do you see?" he asks.

It's a battered wooden bowl. There are a few apples, a banana, some pears, and a mango. I'm pretty sure my mom got the mango on sale because she doesn't usually buy them otherwise.

"A bowl of fruit?" I say.

"Is the fruit alive or dead?" he probes.

I look at it more closely. The apples are red and shiny, and the banana doesn't have any bruises.

"Alive."

He picks up an apple, turning it. "Is it, though? Is it attached to a root system? Is it ingesting nutrients? Water? Those are all signs of life."

"I guess not," I say.

He waves the apple at me. "It actually begins dying the minute you pick it."

Then he goes to the counter and takes a knife from the butcher block. He slices into the apple, exposing a neat row of dark brown seeds.

"Now," he says, touching them with the tip of his knife, "what about these?"

"Dead?" I guess.

"This is trickier. They're dormant, waiting. Bury them in soil. Give them water and sunlight and they'll grow. In a way, they're immortal. And they were inside the apple all along."

I'm kind of blown away.

"I thought science was all experiments and laboratories," I admit.

My grandfather shakes his head. "The most powerful tool of the scientist is observation. Galileo, the father of modern science, observed that Jupiter had moons orbiting it, proving that the Earth was not the center of everything. His observations forced people to think differently about their place in the universe."

Then he looks around and says, "But now that you've mentioned it, I am going to need a laboratory."

"For what?"

"For analyzing the *T. melvinus* when we get it back, of course," he says, like it's obvious. "I need to replicate my results if I'm going to publish."

I think for a minute. Our house isn't exactly huge.

"What about the garage?" I suggest.

We go out to the garage and my grandfather does a slow tour. One half is clear for my mom's car, but the other side is stacked with boxes of props from her shows over the years. There's an old workbench that was my dad's, our bikes, and a freezer. My mom likes to stock up on frozen food before she goes into production on a show.

My grandfather rubs a nonexistent beard on his chin. "Electricity. Decent lighting. It's not climate-controlled, but it could be worse. At least I'm not in the desert like Oppenheimer."

I just look at him.

"Robert Oppenheimer? World War Two?"

"We haven't gotten that far in history," I explain. "We're still at ancient Greece."

"Robert Oppenheimer was a brilliant physicist. He ran the Manhattan Project, which developed the atomic bomb. Oppenheimer tested the atomic bomb in the middle of a desert in New Mexico."

"Wow," I say.

He looks around. "Well, no time like the present. Let's get this place organized."

My grandfather wants to set up the lab around the main electricity outlets, and that means shifting all the prop boxes out of the way. It takes us the better part of two hours to move everything. There's a box of clip lights, and he arranges them around the workbench.

The garage door suddenly rolls open and my mother's car is there. But she can't pull into the garage because of all the boxes. She kills the engine and walks into the garage.

"What are you doing?" she demands.

"We're setting up a lab," I tell her.

"Here? In the garage?"

"So I can continue my research," my grandfather explains.

"Where am I supposed to park my car?" she asks.

"Outside?" I suggest.

"I don't think so," she says.

My grandfather stares at her. "You're standing in the way of scientific discovery."

"I'm standing in the way of birds pooping on my car."

It takes the rest of the afternoon to put everything back.

10
Salk and Oppenheimer

I'm supposed to do a report on a famous histori-
cal figure. But instead of choosing from the likely
suspects—William Shakespeare, Thomas Jefferson,
Harriet Tubman—I use my computer to look up
the names my grandfather's been batting around.
Galileo. Jonas Salk. Robert Oppenheimer.

Galileo's picture is an old oil painting, like
something that should be hanging in the de Young
Museum in San Francisco. He's dressed like he's

in a Shakespeare play and doesn't seem like a real person.

But Salk and Oppenheimer are interesting. Salk looks exactly the way you'd imagine a scientist: glasses, white lab coat, holding test tubes. Nerdy in general.

Oppenheimer is more unexpected: he's handsome, with piercing eyes. He stares broodingly into the camera like an old Hollywood actor. In one shot, he's wearing a hat and has a cigarette dangling from his mouth. I can almost imagine my dad playing his part in a movie. Also, Oppenheimer has a local connection to the Bay Area: he taught at the University of California at Berkeley. My mom is always raving about the theater program there.

I can't help but notice the similarity between the two men: they were both involved in wars where science played a big part in the outcome. Jonas Salk and the War on Polio. Robert Oppenheimer and World War II. Salk found a vaccine that prevented polio, and Oppenheimer helped create the bombs that were dropped on Japan and ended the war.

Oppenheimer's story especially seems like a Hollywood movie. The race against the Germans to create the bomb first. And then there's the photo of one of the bombs exploding with a big mushroom cloud. There's a quote from Oppenheimer, his reaction to the successful testing of the atomic bomb:

"We knew the world would not be the same. A few people laughed. A few people cried. Most people were silent."

I understand how he felt. Like when my grandfather walked through the front door looking like a teenager. Science fiction becoming reality. My mom talks about how she couldn't even have imagined cell phones when she was a kid and now everyone has them. Except me, of course. My parents say I'm too young.

My grandfather comes into my bedroom without knocking. He freezes when he sees the handprints.

"Good grief. What happened to your walls?"

"They're supposed to look that way," I explain.

"That's a style? Whatever happened to a nice wallpaper?"

He points to his face. He's totally breaking out. He's got zits on his forehead and a big red one on his chin.

"Do you have any acne cream?"

"There's some in the bathroom," I tell him, and he follows me in.

"I can't believe I'm seventy-six years old and dealing with pimples again," he grumbles.

I dig through a drawer, find a tube, and hand it to him. He smears some cream on his zits.

"Maybe next time I'll find a cure for acne," he says.

We order Chinese takeout again for dinner. My mom wanted to order sushi, but my grandfather said the person who has the most degrees should get to choose. Since he has two PhDs, he won.

As we eat, I find myself observing my grandfather and mother, like I'm a scientist, an Ellie version of Galileo. For one thing, our whole seating arrangement is different. When it's just my mom and me, we sit next to each other. But my grandfather sits at the head of the counter, like he's the king. Then there's the way they talk to each other—or rather *don't* talk to each other. My grandfather grills my mom with questions I can tell she finds annoying: Does she still have her college transcripts? Would she like to meet with a friend of his in the Stanford biology department to talk about the program? Would she like his help in applying?

She answers him the first few times, but after a while she stops and just looks at her plate, the way a teenager would. I have a sudden realization: even though my mom's a grown-up with her own life, my grandfather still treats her like a kid.

After we finish dinner, I pass out the fortune cookies. My grandfather doesn't look very happy when he reads his fortune.

"What does yours say?" I ask him.

"*You are going to have some new clothes,*" he says.

"Not a bad idea, Dad. Maybe we could get you some clothes with a little style. You look like you shop in the old-man department. I can drive you to the mall," my mom offers.

"There's nothing wrong with my clothes. They're brand-new! I just bought them a few weeks ago after I turned young." To me, he says, "I had to because I shrank."

Then he turns to my mother. "But now that you mention it, I do need to borrow the car, Melissa."

My mom chokes. "*Borrow* the car? I thought you gave up driving."

He gives her a look. "Things have changed. And I have an errand to run."

"Well, you can't drive my car," she replies slowly. "You're not old enough."

He sits up to his full height.

"I certainly am old enough. Would you like to see my driver's license?"

"Dad," she says, her tone placating. "What would happen if you got stopped? You don't exactly *look* like your driver's license."

She's right. With his zits and his long hair

falling out of my ponytail holder, he barely looks old enough to get into a PG-13 movie.

"I won't get stopped."

"I remember how you drive! You always try to pass from the right lane," she says with a groan.

"I get more swing that way," he says. "Simple physics."

"You're going to end up in an accident."

His gaze hardens. "Accident? You want to talk about accidents? Who was the one who wrecked the Volkswagen? Who wrapped it around a tree?"

"It—it wasn't my fault," she stammers. "It was raining. The road was slick. It was dark."

"I'd just paid that car off."

They stare at each other like bulls in the ring.

"I need to borrow the car," he says.

My mom won't let him borrow the car.

"Do you have any idea how many times she

borrowed my car?" he rants on the bus ride to school. He's furious.

"Why don't you just ask her to drive you?" I suggest.

"She won't drive me to the lab," he says. "That rent-a-cop told her he'd press charges if he saw me on the premises again."

"Oh," I say. I see his point.

But on the bus after school, his mood is completely different. He seems almost happy, excited even. When we reach our stop, he doesn't get up.

"Come on. This is us," I tell him.

He doesn't move. "We're getting off at a different stop today."

"We are? Where?"

His eyes gleam.

"My lab."

11
Building Twenty-Four

I take the public bus to school every day, but this time feels completely different—like an adventure.

My grandfather stares out the window. His hair is pulled back in another of my ponytail holders, a purple one.

"Your grandmother loved to ride the bus," he murmurs.

"She did?"

"Yes," he says. "Her dream was for us to take

a bus trip across the country. Stop in little towns. Visit all the tourist traps."

"Did you do it?"

He shakes his head, and something sharp and raw flashes across his face.

"No," he says. "I was always too busy with work."

My grandmother died when I was three. I have a vague memory of walking in on my mother crying in the bathroom.

"Do you miss her?" I ask him.

He blinks fast. "I miss everything about her. I miss her voice. I miss our life together." He swallows. "I miss seeing her walking around in slippers."

"Slippers?"

He shakes his head as if bewildered. "She didn't care about jewelry or perfume or any of that. But she liked a good pair of bedroom slippers. The kind that were furry on the inside. I gave her new ones every year on our anniversary. Silly when you think about it."

But it doesn't sound silly to me. It sounds like love.

o   o   o

We have to switch buses four times. The last bus lets us off on a commercial strip peppered with car dealerships. My grandfather leads me down a side street to a group of buildings. All the buildings are identical—brown brick with dark windows—and they have numbers on their sides. When we reach number twenty-four, my grandfather stops.

"This is it!"

"It is?" I ask. I was expecting something shinier, with glass and metal; this seems pretty ordinary.

But my grandfather seems almost relieved to see the building, like it's an old friend.

"Old number twenty-four," he says.

He hands me a plastic card attached to a lanyard ring.

"What's this for?" I ask.

"To get in. It's my key card." He gestures toward the building. "The security guard will recognize me. It has to be you. I've drawn you a map. The *T. melvinus* is in the freezer in my lab."

I'm a little nervous. "What if the guard sees *me*?"

"I have that all figured out," he assures me. "Just tell him your father works here. Sweet girl like you? He won't suspect a thing."

I swipe the card and slip in a side door without anyone noticing me. I walk down the hall like I have a perfect right to be there, checking my progress by the numbers on the office doors. I'm nearly at my grandfather's lab when a voice stops me dead in my tracks.

"Hey, kid, where do you think you're going?"

I turn around slowly.

A middle-aged security guard is standing there, holding a cup of coffee. He has a walkie-talkie at his waist and a suspicious expression on his face. "I asked you a question, kid."

I use the cover story. "My dad works here."

His shoulders relax. "Oh," he says. "Right."

I give him a little smile and start walking again. Relief pours through my body, the kind of relief you get after passing a test you didn't study for.

"Hey, kid," he calls to me.

I look back at him.

"What's your dad's name?"

I hesitate a moment too long.

Just like that, his eyes narrow and he shakes his head. "We had another one of you crazy kids sneaking in here the other day. Let's take a walk to my office," he says.

In the split second before he reaches me, I see my future: in the back of a police car.

I start running.

"Stop!" he shouts.

I fly out of the building toward the bushes where my grandfather is waiting. When he sees me running, he starts running, too.

We hide out in a tiny taco place until the coast is clear. Then we catch a bus home.

"I'm proud of you," my grandfather says to me.

"But I didn't get it," I tell him.

He shakes his head. "Scientists fail all the time.

You tried. That's what counts. You have to keep at it. Just like Marie Curie."

It feels like a compliment.

"What did she do?"

"Marie Curie won a Nobel for her work on radiation."

"Do you think I'll ever win a Nobel?" I ask.

"Of course you will," he says without a second's hesitation.

And I believe him.

12
Raisinets

It's Saturday night and my mom has a date with Ben. They're going to drop off my grandfather and me at the movie theater, grab dinner, and pick us up on the way home.

I watch her as she gets ready. Her hair is blue now. She changed it a few days ago, and when my grandfather saw it, he shook his head and asked if she was working for the circus.

"How do I look?" my mom asks me.

She models her outfit: a purple skirt, a silver-sequined top, a wide black vinyl belt, and tall pleather boots. Sometimes it's a little hard having a mom who's hipper than you are.

"Great!"

The doorbell rings and my mom says what she always says: "Tell Ben I'll be down in a minute."

Ben is standing on the front porch with a bouquet of carnations. Even though he and my mom are way past the flowers stage, he brings her flowers every time they have a date. I think it's sweet.

"How's it hanging?" he asks, which is what he always says.

My mom says that the thing she loves most about Ben is that there's no drama, which is a funny thing for a drama teacher to say. I like that he doesn't try to be my dad. He's just Ben.

"She's still getting ready. She'll be down in a few minutes," I say, although he and I both know she'll probably be a while.

Ben's eyes crinkle and he says half-jokingly, "I'd wait for your mother forever."

He's asked my mother to marry him twice, and both times she's told him she wasn't ready. I once overheard her tell Bernadette she was scared of making a mistake again.

My grandfather walks into the hall and gives Ben an icy look. In addition to his usual polyester pants and button-up shirt, he's put on a crimson tie. He told me he always dresses up when he goes to the movies.

"You must be Ellie's cousin," Ben says. "Melvin, right? I'm Ben."

My grandfather doesn't say anything; he just gives Ben a hostile look.

Ben nods at my grandfather's tie. "So you're a tie guy, huh? That's pretty classic."

"Classic" is definitely a good way to describe my grandfather.

My mother walks in.

"You look beautiful, Lissa," he says.

She points to her top. "Not too sparkly?"

Ben smiles. "It's perfect."

"You need a shawl," my grandfather tells her.

"What?" my mom asks.

"All that skin," my grandfather insists. "It's like something a teenager would wear. You need a shawl."

My mom's mouth opens and closes in fury.

After the movie, my grandfather and I wait outside to get picked up. The nightly parade is going on: girls walk with arms linked by boys who pretend not to notice them, while other boys whiz by on skateboards.

"Idiot," my grandfather comments when a skateboarder executes a neat flip. "One good fall and he'll need a knee replacement."

He shakes his box of Raisinets. He's already worked his way through a bag of popcorn, a box of gummy bears, nachos, a root beer, and a milk shake.

"They're not as good as they used to be," he complains.

"They're just chocolate-covered raisins," I say. "How can they taste different?"

"They were just better. Like a lot of things."

"Like what?"

"Like movies. That one was a piece of garbage. Back in my day, they made quality movies."

It was an animated fairy tale and I didn't like it much, either. I'd really wanted to see a Japanese horror movie, but it was sold out.

I like scary films; I'm not a big fairy-tale fan. Mostly because I always wonder about the *after* part of happily-ever-after. Like in "The Three Little Pigs." What happened after the third pig cooked the wolf in the pot? Did he hold a funeral and let the wolf's friends know? Or with "Cinderella." Sure, she got the prince, but what about the stepsisters? They were still her family. Did she have to see them at Thanksgiving dinner? Talk about awkward.

"Looks like Halloween is early this year," my grandfather says, gesturing to a group of goth boys standing in line. I find myself looking for Raj, but he's not there.

A sweet-looking old lady pushing an equally elderly man in a wheelchair passes us. The man is hunched over and holding a cane. He's wearing dark polyester pants, a button-up shirt, a navy-blue blazer, and loafers with dark socks.

He's dressed just like my grandfather.

"Do you see that, Ellie? Growing old is a terrible disease. Things you take for granted, you lose. Your ability to walk. Your vision. Your hearing. Even being able to go to the bathroom."

"Huh?"

He gives me a knowing look. "Everything falls apart when you get old. Believe me, you don't want to know how many times I used to get up during the night to pee."

I nod my head in agreement. That is way too much information.

"But that's not even the worst of it. They stick you away in nursing homes and assisted-living facilities just because you're old."

Kind of like middle school.

"Then do you know what happens?" He pauses

dramatically. "Everybody around you starts dying! Heart attacks! Strokes! Cancer! People you've known your whole life are just gone! People you love! Can you imagine how painful that is?"

I think of Brianna.

There's a chorus of laughter from a bunch of kids as a boy kicks his skateboard in the air.

"I'd rather be dead than old," he declares.

Then he crumples the Raisinets box.

"I'm still hungry," he says.

13
Ankh

Things are a little different with my grandfather living with us. The pullout couch in the den is permanently pulled out, and our antique bookshelves have been emptied and turned into an open dresser. The whole room has a gamy, boy-sock, locker-room smell. My mother has taken to spraying air freshener when he isn't looking.

My grandfather has a few quirks. He's always ready to go somewhere a good half hour before it's time to leave. He drinks a cup of hot tea every day because it's "good for digestion." He has a thing about the trash.

"You should put the trash cans out at night," he tells my mom.

"I like to do it in the morning," she says.

"What if you forget?"

My mother grits her teeth. "I won't forget."

"You might," he says. "And you'll end up with two weeks of trash in your cans. Then you'll have a real problem."

There's no need to try to figure out what he really means, the way there sometimes is with girls; he's blunt. And he always does what he says he will, so when he doesn't show up at the end of the school day, I start to get nervous.

I'm waiting for him at our usual meeting spot— the flagpole in front of the school. The stream of kids rushing by slows to a trickle, but he's still nowhere in sight. I know he wouldn't just leave me here. Then I remember Nicole talking about old people wandering off. Even though my grandfather has a teenager's body, he still has a seventy-six-year-old brain.

I check by his locker and his last class of the day, but nothing. Now I'm getting really worried, so I go to one of the boys' bathrooms and shout in the door.

"Melvin?"

Raj walks out.

"I think you have the wrong bathroom," he says lightly.

"Is Melvin in there?"

"Uh, you want me to check?"

"Will you?" I ask.

He's back in a moment. He shakes his head. "Nope, no Melvin."

"Where is he?" I ask. Something like panic fills me.

Raj says, "I'll help you look for him. He's around here somewhere, I'm sure."

Raj checks all the boys' bathrooms and the locker room, but he's nowhere.

It's only when we're going past my locker that I see it: a note sticking to the metal.

I'm in detention.
—Melvin

Raj offers to wait with me. We sit on a bench outside the detention room. He's fun to talk to.

"Your cousin's a little strange," he says.

I look at him.

"I mean, the way he dresses and all? Those polyester pants? He reminds me of my grandfather."

If he only knew.

"Uh, yeah. It's just kind of his style, I guess," I say.

"Huh," he says.

He's got a dangling earring in his right ear. It looks like a hieroglyphic.

"That's Egyptian, right?"

"It's an ankh. It's the Egyptian symbol for life," he explains.

"Cool," I say. "So you kind of have a thing for ancient Egyptian stuff?"

"Kind of. Did you know they left in the heart?"

"What?"

"When they made mummies, they took out all the organs but they left in the heart."

"Why'd they do that?"

His eyes are serious. "They believed that the heart did the thinking."

The detention door bangs open and kids flood out. My grandfather storms up to us, red in the face, his hair bouncing everywhere.

"What happened?" I ask him.

"I used the facilities," he says.

He's not making any sense.

"The facilities?"

"The toilet!" my grandfather snaps. "I went to the toilet during class without getting a bathroom pass! Apparently that's a state crime!"

A bunch of kids who were in detention with

my grandfather shoot him high-five signs when they pass.

One laughs and says, "Fight the power, bro!"

My grandfather gives him a withering look.

"You're supposed to take a hall pass when you go to the bathroom," I explain.

"By the way, the teacher who sentenced me should not be teaching history. She's twenty-two if she's a day." He shakes his head in disgust. "What does she know about anything?"

"Maybe next time you should just take the pass," Raj suggests.

"I prefer to keep my dignity," he announces.

As he marches off, hair flying, I realize my mom's wrong.

He does have a flair for drama.

14

Cheese

My mom gets home from school early. When she walks in the door, she's carrying two big bags of groceries.

"Rehearsals are going great, so I let everyone have the day off! I thought I'd make us dinner," she enthuses. She adds, "I feel like I've been neglecting you lately, Ellie."

She spends the rest of the afternoon in the kitchen. When we go in for dinner, it looks like a

tornado hit the place: dirty bowls and measuring cups are piled in the sink, and flour is all over the counter. She must have used every single pot in the house.

"Dinner is served!" she announces, and places our plates in front of us with a flourish.

There's a breaded, fried, patty-like thing lying in the middle of each plate. Next to it is some singed asparagus.

My grandfather and I both take a bite.

"So?" my mom asks. "What do you think?"

It's mushy, with a weird texture, and has way too much pepper.

My grandfather makes a face. "What is this supposed to be?"

"Fried eggplant," she says.

His answer is decisive. "Nope. Don't like it."

She looks at me. "Do you like it?"

I shake my head.

Her shoulders sag in defeat.

The eggplant goes in the trash and we order Chinese.

o   o   o

My grandfather and I are in the kitchen the next day after school, and he's complaining about my mother's cooking.

"If she had paid as much attention to chemistry as she did to this theater nonsense, she'd be a good cook," he says. He exaggerates the word "theater" so that it sounds like *thee-a-tah*.

"Chemistry? What does that have to do with anything?"

He looks at me. "Cooking is science."

"It is?" It has always seemed so arty to me.

"It's all basic chemistry," he says. "In fact, science has its fingerprints all over the kitchen."

He opens the refrigerator and takes out a block of cheese, waves it.

"Louis Pasteur discovered a way to kill bacteria in drinks: pasteurization, or heating at high temperatures. It was practically a miracle at the time! That's why we can drink milk and eat cheese without getting sick."

86

I'd had no idea that cheese was a miracle.

"I like to cook," I tell him.

"Of course you do," he says, as if it's perfectly obvious. "You take after me."

Maybe I do take after him.

He claps his hands. "Let's make dinner."

"What should we make?" I ask. Most of my recipes are breakfast-oriented.

He looks in the refrigerator and then goes to the green wooden recipe box on the windowsill above the sink. The recipe box belonged to my grandmother. Sometimes when my mother's had a bad day, she'll pull out the little cards and read them. She says she just likes to look at her mother's handwriting.

My grandfather ticks through the recipes with a critical eye, then pulls one out.

"Ah, yes, this will do nicely," he says.

I look at the recipe card. It has stains on it like it's been used a lot. In perfect loopy cursive, it reads:

Coq au Vin (Melvin's favorite)

He adds, "And it's French like Louis Pasteur."

"The only French food I've ever eaten is French fries," I confess.

"You can't go wrong with French food," he assures me. "It's the best cuisine in the world."

We settle in at the kitchen counter, working side by side. He's a tidy cook; he cleans up as he goes along, just like me. He shows me how to cut the carrots. How to brown the chicken with bacon. How to combine everything and simmer with red wine. I start to see how the kitchen is kind of like a laboratory. The glass bowls. The measuring spoons. The gas flame on a stove is like a Bunsen burner. When you think about it, even cooks' white aprons are similar to the white coats that scientists wear.

But maybe there's also a little magic in cooking, taking all the plain old ingredients and turning them into comfort and memory. Because when my mom walks in the door, she sniffs the air expectantly.

"Something smells wonderful," she says.

"We cooked dinner!" I say.

My grandfather holds out a plate to her.

"Is that—" she starts to ask.

My grandfather finishes her sentence. "Your mother's coq au vin."

She takes a bite and her face turns up in a smile.

"It tastes exactly the way I remember it," she murmurs.

His eyes shine. "Yes," he says.

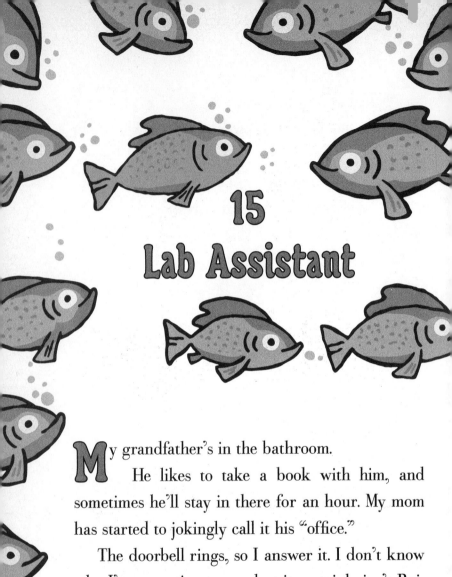

15
Lab Assistant

My grandfather's in the bathroom.

He likes to take a book with him, and sometimes he'll stay in there for an hour. My mom has started to jokingly call it his "office."

The doorbell rings, so I answer it. I don't know who I'm expecting to see, but it certainly isn't Raj.

"Hey, Ellie," he says. He's wearing his usual black outfit.

90

I smile back weakly. "Uh, hi."

We stand there for a minute.

Raj shifts on his feet. "So, are you going to invite me in?"

I stand back. "Oh, sure. Come in!"

He walks into our foyer and looks around the hallway. "Is Melvin home?"

Confusion floods me. "You're here to see Melvin?"

Before he can answer, the toilet flushes and my grandfather emerges from the bathroom.

"You're late," my grandfather informs him.

"Yo, Dr. Sagarsky," he says.

I'm dumbfounded. "You *told* him?" I ask my grandfather.

"Why not?" My grandfather waves a hand at Raj's earring. "Who'd believe *him* anyway?"

"I almost didn't believe it," Raj admits. "But it's amazing what you can find on the Internet."

He holds out a piece of paper.

It's a printout of an old newspaper article. It says: *Fresno Boy Wins Central Valley Science Fair.* Next to the article is a photo of my grandfather with the caption "Melvin Sagarsky, age 15." He looks exactly like he does now, except with a crew cut.

"I think I like you better with short hair," Raj says to my grandfather.

"Try being bald for thirty years, and see how fast you cut your hair when you get it back," my grandfather says.

"By the way, did you know you have a fan club in Finland?"

My grandfather preens. "They have T-shirts now."

"I saw that," Raj says. "I'll buy one when they come in black."

"Let's get to work," my grandfather says.

"Work?" I echo.

"He hired me," Raj answers.

I turn to my grandfather. "You're paying him?"

My grandfather looks unconcerned. "I have plenty of money. Start saving now. Compound interest is a wonderful thing."

"But why him?"

"He has all the qualifications I require in a lab assistant."

"Oh," I say, and feel oddly hurt. I thought *I* was his lab assistant.

Raj gives me an ironic smile. "An older brother with a car."

My grandfather has a plan to get into building twenty-four, and it feels like it's straight out of a spy movie.

We'll go at night when there are fewer people around—just a few lab assistants running experiments. And the security guard, of course. But my grandfather has that covered this time. Raj will ring the front bell to create a diversion. While the security guard is distracted, my grandfather will use his key card to get in the back door and grab the *T. melvinus*. Raj's brother will drive the getaway car.

"It's a perfect plan," my grandfather says. "And it's much easier than taking all those buses."

He picks a night that my mother has late rehearsals so she won't know about our criminal activity. I'm holed up in my bedroom looking at microscopic photos of bacteria on the Internet. I want to learn more about the whole cheese thing. Bacteria are strangely beautiful. Some are cylindrical, some are coiled, some are spheres. They have impressive names: *Escherichia coli. Bacillus megaterium. Helicobacter pylori.* There's even a bacterium named after Pasteur: *Pasteurella multocida.* I think about my grandfather and the jellyfish and feel a little jealous. I kind of want something named after me.

My bedroom door slams open, and my grandfather is standing there dressed head to toe in black. He's raided my mother's closet and is wearing her favorite black T-shirt and a black leather jacket from her "punk phase" in college. Even his legs are in black.

"Are those Mom's leggings?" I ask him.

"Is that what they're called?" He hurries me along. "Time to go. Our ride is here."

A car is idling at the curb, Raj's brother behind the wheel. We get in and Raj introduces everyone.

"This is my brother, Ananda," Raj says. "This is Melvin and Ellie."

Ananda just nods and cranks up the radio.

"By the way," Raj says, "I have to be home by nine-thirty. It's a school night."

"This shouldn't take long," my grandfather says, holding up our picnic cooler. "We'll just grab the *T. melvinus* and go."

The trip is a lot faster than taking the bus. When we arrive at building twenty-four, there's only one car in the lot. We cruise by and then park down the street.

My grandfather hands a ski mask to Raj and pulls one over his head.

"Seriously?" Raj asks.

"They have security cameras, you know."

"Great," Raj mutters.

They take off into the darkness, and Ananda and I sit in silence, listening to the radio.

His eyes meet mine in the rearview mirror.

"Do you do this sort of thing a lot?" he asks me.

"Just once before," I tell him.

We don't have to wait long. My grandfather and Raj run up to the car and jump in.

"Drive!" my grandfather shouts, and we take off.

"Did you get it?" I ask my grandfather.

"I couldn't even get in!" he barks.

Raj looks at me. "His key card doesn't work anymore. They must have deactivated it."

My grandfather grumbles the whole way home.

When they drop us off, Raj leans out the window and calls to my grandfather, "You still have to pay me."

The next morning, my mother asks, "Have you seen my black leggings? I can't find them anywhere."

"Check with Grandpa," I tell her.

She narrows her eyes at me. "I don't even want to know."

16
Slippers

It's eight o'clock on Saturday morning and my grandfather is pacing the front hall. He's been up and dressed since six-thirty. I know because I'm the same way: I get up early even on Saturdays. Maybe it's a scientist thing because my mom is all about sleeping late.

"When are we going?" he calls out, his voice ringing through the house.

He wants to get his own computer and a few

other things from his apartment. My mom promised him we would go over the weekend.

"Rome is going to fall again by the time you people get moving!"

My mom stomps down the hall in her pajamas. She is not an early bird.

"Would you just relax?" she snaps. "I haven't even had my coffee."

It's after ten when we finally get in the car and head to my grandfather's apartment. I look out the window as we drive along the highway. We pass a sign for a biotech company. It says WE ARE THE FUTURE OF MEDICAL RESEARCH and has a picture of a bacterium I recognize.

"Look! It's *Escherichia coli*!" I say to my grandfather.

"So it is," he says.

"What's that?" my mother asks.

"It's a bacterium," I tell her.

She gives my grandfather a quick glance. "Are you brainwashing my daughter?"

"Your daughter's interested in science. She shows great aptitude. You should encourage her."

I feel a flush of pride. Maybe this part of me—the science part—was there all along, like the seeds of an apple. I just needed someone to water it, help it grow. Someone like my grandfather.

When we get off at the exit, my grandfather says to my mom, "Drive by the old place."

He lives in an apartment building now, but when my grandmother was alive, they lived in a house. This is where my mother grew up.

My mom parks next to a Craftsman-style house with big blooms of lavender out front. There's a tricycle in the driveway.

My grandfather says, "Your mother's lavender is still there."

"Looks like they put in new windows," my mom observes.

"Your mother would be thrilled," he says, and for some reason they both laugh.

I don't know if the memories I have of my

grandmother are actually real, or if they've just been told to me so many times. How she wore chopsticks in her hair and how she stitched up the hole I chewed in my baby blanket so that it looked perfectly new again. What I do remember is a feeling: people shouting less and laughing more when she was around.

"It's nice to see a family living in the old place," my mother says. "Life goes on."

My grandfather just stares at the house.

I haven't been up in my grandfather's apartment for a while now.

"It's like walking into 1975," my mother murmurs under her breath.

The furniture is old. There's a yellowy-orange velour couch that has a plastic cover on it and a matching orange recliner. I remember playing with the lounging chair when I was little, tipping the wooden handle and lying back.

"Seriously, Dad," my mom says, running her hand along the couch. "Maybe you should think about a new couch."

"I like that couch," he says. "I don't want to get rid of it. Your mother picked it out."

There are piles of scientific periodicals and little china figurines of fat-faced children that belonged to my grandmother. Everything has a thin layer of dust on it.

I wander over to the kitchen. Sitting on the counter is a huge cookie jar in the shape of a brown owl. I take off the lid, peek inside. Instead of cookies, there are packets of soy sauce. I guess that solves the mystery of where all the soy sauce ends up.

My grandfather goes to a rolltop desk and opens it. He starts gathering papers and notebooks.

"Ellie," he orders, "there's a suitcase in the bedroom closet. Get it for me."

"Okay," I say.

The bedroom is just like I remember, the furniture painted white with dark knobs. The bedspread is flowery and quilted and has a sheen to it. There are two dressers, his-and-hers. My grandmother's dresser looks like it's been dusted, and there's a vase with dried lavender on top of it. But my grandfather's dresser is crowded with stuff: a jelly jar full of coins, a framed wedding photo of him and my grandmother, piles of receipts, pens with the logo of a local bank, toothpicks, dental floss, two pairs of glasses, random buttons, and folded cloth handkerchiefs.

In the middle of the mess is an old, faded greeting card propped up next to a teddy bear. It says *Happy Anniversary* in flowery script on the outside. I recognize the handwriting inside the card; it's the same as in the recipe box:

> To Melvin—
> Happy one-year anniversary!
> Your blushing bride,
> Mona

I go to the closet and take the suitcase out. It tumbles to the floor, the top falling open. As I'm zipping it up, something nearby catches my eye. I feel like a scientist making a discovery, except it's not a vaccine or a bomb. It's a pair of fuzzy pink bedroom slippers.

They're tucked neatly under the bed, as if waiting for their owner to slip them on again.

17
Law of Friendship

Heads turn when my grandfather comes storming across the lunch court.

He hates to do laundry and has started to borrow from my mom's closet when he's running low on clean clothes.

Today he's wearing her hot-pink sweatpants and *Phantom of the Opera* T-shirt.

"I can't believe *this* is on the reading list," he huffs, and holds up a book—*The Catcher in the Rye.*

"What's wrong with it?" I ask.

He starts eating my leftover chips.

"All this Holden kid does is whine. He should just get a job."

"I haven't read it yet," I say, although my mom talks about it all the time. Holden Caulfield is one of her heroes.

"You don't need to," my grandfather says. "You should be reading the classics."

"I think it *is* a classic."

"Please. I highly doubt Newton wasted his time on this drivel."

"Newton? You mean like the cookie?"

"No! Isaac Newton! The father of modern physics!"

My eyes are drawn past him to the lunch line, where Brianna is waiting to pay. She's with a bunch of volleyball players. It must be some kind of spirit day because they're wearing their team shirts and have put on silly face paint.

"Isaac Newton established the three laws of motion," my grandfather says, and points to the plastic fork on his tray. "The first law states that an object at rest will stay at rest and an object in motion will stay in motion *unless* an external force acts upon it."

He smacks the fork and it bounces.

"Which, in this case, was my hand," he explains.

Was it science that happened to Brianna and me? Were we two objects in motion, hurtling through space, and then an external force—middle school, volleyball, life?—hit us?

As my grandfather drones on, I wonder: shouldn't there be a "law of friendship," that if you're friends with someone practically your whole life, you can't just suddenly stop and change directions without the other person?

My grandfather's voice shakes me back to the present.

"And that is Newton's laws of motion in a nutshell," he finishes. "You just learned physics, Ellie. Don't you feel smarter?"

I stare at him.

Raj walks up to the table and eyes my grandfather.

"Love the new look, doc," he says.

Speaking of looks, Raj has a new piercing: a silver ball under his lower lip.

My grandfather shakes his head.

"Why do you do that to yourself? You're going to get a terrible infection. Have you heard of staph?"

"It's self-expression," Raj says.

"Self-expression? Really?" my grandfather mocks. "I'll be sure to alert Harvard."

Raj comes home with us after school. We sit around my puzzle at the kitchen table. My grandfather's been working on it lately. Sometimes when we're watching TV, he'll abruptly walk over to the puzzle table, pick up a piece, and click it in. It's like he's been thinking about it the whole time.

My grandfather gives Raj an assessing look. "Do you know any underworld types who could help us break into building twenty-four?"

Raj stares at him. "Why would I know someone like that?"

"I just assumed," he says, waving a hand at Raj's black clothes, the metal piercings.

Raj gives him a funny look.

"Well, start thinking of a way to get in," he orders Raj. "You're on the clock."

Then he grabs his copy of *The Catcher in the Rye* and stomps out of the kitchen.

Raj turns to me. "Where'd he go?"

"The bathroom. He'll probably be in there for a while."

I heat up some burritos. It turns out that Raj loves them as much as I do. We settle down at the kitchen counter to eat and make lists of how to break into the lab. Our ideas are silly—mailing ourselves to the lab as packages or parachuting in.

The strange thing is, it all feels so cozy. I wonder if this was what it was like for Oppenheimer and his team of scientists when they were working on the bomb. Did they sit around eating burritos and coming up with ideas?

"We need a name," I tell Raj.

He cocks an eyebrow and I explain.

"Like they did with the Manhattan Project. When they were creating the atomic bomb."

We try out a few names (the Melvin Sagarsky Project, the Jellyfish Project, the Raj and Ellie Are Totally Cool Project). And then Raj snaps his fingers.

"I got it," he says, pointing to his plate. "The Burrito Project."

My grandfather explodes into the kitchen, shouting, "They closed my email account!"

"Who?"

He's outraged. "My email account at the lab! Someone closed my account. I can't access it anymore!"

"That's a bummer," Raj says. "But you can just set up a new email account, you know. They're free. I did one for my grandmother."

But my grandfather is beside himself. "It's not that! All of my contacts are in there! The diver who found the *T. melvinus*! I don't even know his last name! All I know is that his name is Billy and he's Australian. Do you have any idea how many Australian Billys there are?"

Raj and I share a look.

"A lot?" I guess.

My grandfather fumes. "I bet it was that Terrence character, the one in the flashy suit. He kept telling me to move my stuff out of the lab. Little upstart. Who does he think he is? I have years of experience on him! Decades!" He waves *The Catcher in the Rye* in the air like a weapon. "He's just like this Holden character! A phony!"

There's a beat of silence.

Raj says, "You're reading *The Catcher in the Rye*? That's a really good book."

18
Degrees

Ben's taking us all out for dinner. My grandfather insists on wearing a jacket and tie, even though we're just going to the Mexican place.

"Quite the fashion statement," my mother says.

"What? Don't people dress up for dinner anymore?" he counters.

When we get to the restaurant, Ben's not there yet, so we grab a table at the back. I love the burritos at this place.

"Real big spender, huh?" my grandfather says, looking around at the linoleum floor, the plastic flower arrangements. "We should have just gone to a Chinese place."

"They give free refills on chips here," I tell him.

"Ooh la la," my grandfather says. "How fancy!"

My mother glares at him, and then the bell on the door rings and her face lights up. Ben walks in, wearing a dark suit and a tie.

"You see?" my grandfather mutters. "He's wearing a jacket and tie!"

"Sorry I'm late," Ben apologizes. "Client meeting."

The waitress comes and takes our order. I get my usual—a burrito. My mother and Ben both get the fish tacos. My grandfather gets a cheese quesadilla, three beef tacos, chicken fajitas, a side of rice and beans, and an extra side of guacamole.

When the waitress brings our meals, my grandfather's order takes up half the table. He starts eating immediately, working his way methodically through his food. Ben seems a little envious.

"I was like that at your age," Ben tells my grandfather, patting his belly. "Now I have to watch myself."

My grandfather just looks at him and stuffs another forkful in his mouth.

"So how are you liking your new school, Melvin?" Ben asks my grandfather.

My grandfather doesn't even look up. He's got the whole sullen-teenager thing down pat.

My mom clears her throat.

"I'm unimpressed," he finally says. "I find the curriculum rather lacking."

Ben looks taken aback. "Really?"

"Melvin was in the gifted-and-talented program at his old school," my mom quickly improvises. "He's used to more of a challenge."

My grandfather burps loudly.

"Melvin!" my mother hisses.

"What?" he says.

"Don't be rude!"

"I'm not being rude; it's the bacteria."

My mother looks at him. "What?"

"There are bacteria in your stomach that help digest food. During the process, gas is released," he explains. "That's why you burp."

"And fart?" I ask.

He nods. "Exactly."

My mother groans, but Ben laughs and says, "Seems like *you're* learning something at school, Melvin."

"Where did *you* go to school?" my grandfather asks Ben bluntly.

"Melvin," my mother says in a warning voice.

"Let him ask questions," Ben says good-naturedly. "I like an inquiring mind. I did under-grad at Harvard."

"I've heard of it," my grandfather says, twisting the ring on his finger.

"And I got my PhD at MIT."

My grandfather appears vaguely impressed. "Who do you work for now?"

"A start-up here in Silicon Valley," Ben says. "We make video games."

"Video games? You went to Harvard and MIT and *that's* what you're doing now?"

Ben nods and picks up a chip.

My grandfather shakes his head. "What a complete waste of degrees," he says.

"It's an incredibly artistic field," my mom says, defending Ben.

"Oh, well, if it's artistic, then I'm sure it's *wonderful*," my grandfather says.

My mother rubs her forehead like she's having a migraine.

"So have you been married before?" my grandfather asks Ben.

Ben blinks. "No."

"Any kids?"

"Not that I'm aware of," Ben answers.

"I think that's enough, Melvin," my mother warns in a low voice.

"Just a minute," my grandfather says. "I have one last question for you."

"Yes?" Ben asks.

"Just what are your intentions—"

My mother's shout cuts him off. "Melvin!"

Then my grandfather points to Ben's plate.

"—with that last taco?" my grandfather finishes with a smirk.

19
Genie in the Bottle

My mom takes me grocery shopping with her. It's a little bit of a fight to get inside Safeway, with all the protesters. People are always outside holding signs for some cause or proposition on the local ballot. They all jockey for space with the pet-rescue society and the Salvation Army.

We get a cart and by the time we're done, it's piled high. We never bought this much food when it was just the two of us. We can stretch a pint of ice cream over a week, but my grandfather will finish it in a single sitting.

"Your grandfather is eating me out of house and home," she says as we wait in the checkout line.

"At least you don't have to pay a babysitter," I point out.

"And he's driving me nuts with the whole trash can thing."

I look at her. "Did you know that he has a fan club?"

"He has a fan club?"

I nod. "In Finland."

She shakes her head in bewilderment. "Unbelievable. Does he drive them crazy, too?"

"I like having him around," I tell her.

"I've noticed," she replies. "You two are like Rosencrantz and Guildenstern. By the way, there's a bunch of extra paint at the theater if you and Brianna want to do your handprints."

I hesitate. "I don't know if we're going to do the handprint thing anymore."

My mom doesn't say anything; she just gives me a long look.

Then she changes the subject. "It's kind of funny that you're interested in all this science stuff. I hated it. Your grandfather used to drag me to his lab when I was a kid."

"What did you do?" I ask.

"I washed test tubes."

It sounds like fun to me. "Were there any cool experiments?"

"It was all completely boring; that was the problem," my mom explains. "No emotions, no excitement, no drama!"

But I know she's wrong about this. "There's lots of drama in science."

"Really? A bunch of boring people standing around in white lab coats?"

"They aren't boring! They're passionate! Like you're always talking about!"

She raises an eyebrow, and I want to make her understand.

"We were losing World War Two, and Oppenheimer and all these scientists created the atomic bomb and saved the day. That's pretty dramatic, right?"

She gives a grudging nod.

"Or like with Salk. Kids were dying from the polio epidemic, and everybody was scared. Jonas Salk and this whole crew of scientists believed it must be possible to stop it, and so they worked night and day to find a vaccine. And they did it!"

Something in her face softens a little. "You sure know a lot about this," she says.

I guess I do.

"Still, those stories could use some romance," my mom points out.

"There's lots of romance," I insist.

She looks confused. "Really? Who are they in love with?"

"Possibility."

O   O   O

We load the groceries into the car, and then I push the cart back to the store. I slow as I pass the pro-testers' tables, surprised to see my science teacher behind one. There's a sign taped to the table that says ABOLISH NUCLEAR WEAPONS NOW.

"Hi, Ellie," Mr. Ham says.

It's always funny running into teachers when they're not in their school clothes. Mr. Ham's not wearing a tie today. Instead, he's got on a T-shirt that says NO NUKES, a pair of shorts, and bright blue sneakers.

"Doing a little grocery shopping?" he asks me.

"With my mom. What's this?"

"Oh, I volunteer for this organization a couple of times a year." He puts on his "volunteer" face. "Could I interest you in a brochure, Miss Cruz?"

"Do I get extra credit?" I ask.

"Absolutely," he says with a smile.

I recognize the mushroom-cloud picture on the brochure. But there's another picture, of a bombed-out city, next to it. The caption reads: "Hiroshima: the war begins."

"But the atomic bomb ended the war," I say, confused.

Mr. Ham gives me a questioning look. "Did it? Or will it start a larger war? Because we're always going to be waiting for the next bomb to drop. You can't put the genie back in the bottle."

I hear a horn honking. My mom's pulled up to the curb.

"Looks like your ride's here," he says.

After I get into the car, I look back at Mr. Ham. He gives me a little wave.

When I go to get breakfast the next morning, my mom and grandfather are already in the kitchen.

"I thought I told you not to put the trash cans out at night!" my mom says furiously.

"What?" he says. "You should be happy I took them out."

"There is a reason I told you not to do that," she says. "Come with me."

We follow her outside. The cans are next to the curb and the lids have been knocked open. Gross, rotting, stinky trash has been strewn all across the street by some enthusiastic animal.

"We have raccoons!" She narrows her eyes. "Maybe your Finnish fan club can help you clean it up!"

Then she stomps off.

20
Mad Scientist

Halloween's coming up fast. This is the first year I won't be going trick-or-treating. The town likes to keep the older kids off the street, so there's a dance party at the youth center on Halloween night.

In science class, Mr. Ham is already getting into the spirit of things. His tie has skeletons on it.

"Are you going to the Halloween party?" I ask Momo.

She shakes her head. "I have to take my little brother trick-or-treating."

I ask Raj at lunch if he's going.

"Sure I am," he says. "Halloween is the best night of the whole year. You get to dress up."

"Please," my grandfather snorts. "It's Halloween for you every day."

I decide that I want to go, but I don't know what to wear. For the past few Halloweens, Brianna and I have coordinated our costumes. But I don't need a PhD to know that she and I won't be doing the whole buddy-costume thing this year. My mom offers to take me to the high school so I can look through the wardrobe closet at the theater.

"I've got a great hippie costume from my production of *Hair,*" she tells me as I rummage through the racks of clothes.

I shake my head. "It's not me."

For my parents, costumes are no big thing. It's part of their job, like a uniform.

But I think what you wear on Halloween is important. It says something about you—who you are and what you want to be. There's got to be a reason so many girls go around dressed as princesses and witches.

I dig through and when I see it, I know instantly that it's perfect. I don't know why I didn't think of it in the first place.

On Halloween night, I hole up in my room, getting dressed. When I make my grand entrance, my mom and Ben are already sitting on the front porch, big bowls of candy on their laps. They're in costume, too.

She's dressed as Little Bo Peep, complete with a crinoline skirt and a shepherdess's crook. But it's Ben's costume that makes it: he's dressed up as the sheep. He's wearing a fluffy white costume and has a sign on his chest that says I'M NOT LOST. I JUST HATE ASKING FOR DIRECTIONS.

"Baa," Ben says.

I laugh, but my grandfather shakes his head like he doesn't understand.

"Are you supposed to be Einstein?" Ben asks me.

126

I'm wearing a white lab coat and a crazy bushy white wig. I've got thick glasses, and I'm holding a test tube filled with glow-in-the-dark green paint.

"Just your basic mad scientist," I tell him.

My grandfather told me he was too old for Halloween, so he's wearing his usual outfit: polyester pants, button-up shirt and cardigan, black socks, and loafers. I convinced him to wear a neon-orange ponytail holder so he would look a little Halloweeny.

"Don't tell me," my mom teases him. "You're supposed to be an old man."

My grandfather scowls at her. "Ha ha."

Ben greets trick-or-treaters while my mom takes us over to the youth center. We wait for Raj outside and check out the costumes. There are a lot of sexy-looking angels and devils. My favorite is two kids who have dressed up as Dorothy and the Tin Woodman, except they've switched it up: the boy is Dorothy and the girl is the Tin Woodman.

My grandfather asks, "Do you think they'll have caramel apples?"

"The flyer said there would be food. Why?"

"I haven't had a caramel apple in years," he says.

Raj walks up, and he's not wearing any black at all. In fact, he's wearing green chino pants and a pink polo shirt that has the collar turned up. A white sweater is tied around his shoulders, and his belt has whales on it. He's traded in his black Doc Martens for brown loafers with no socks, and he's dyed his hair blond and combed it back. I would hardly even recognize him except for his piercings.

"What are you supposed to be?"

He sticks his hands in his pockets and slouches.

"Preppy," he says.

I laugh.

My grandfather shifts awkwardly. "So, what do we do now?"

"I think we're supposed to have fun," I say.

"Fun? What a waste of time," he grumbles.

We pay our money and head inside. It's dark and music thumps out of the stereo. Black lights and orange Day-Glo decorations are everywhere. There are strobe lights and even a fog machine.

My grandfather heads straight for the food and we trail after him.

"No caramel apples. It's a sad state of affairs when you can't get a caramel apple on Halloween," he grouses.

I feel a twinge of unease now that I'm here. I'm not much of a dancer, even though I've taken ballet, tap, and jazz (my parents are big believers that all theater people should know how to dance). It's the whole being-onstage thing. I always freeze up or overthink the steps and how I look doing them. It's hard to relax when everyone is watching you.

A bouncy pop song comes on.

"Wanna dance?" Raj asks.

"My dancing days are over," my grandfather replies.

"Not you," Raj clarifies. "Ellie."

I feel my cheeks heat up.

"Sure," I whisper.

I don't know if it's the music, or the dark, or

the safety of the costume, but the nervousness I usually feel when stepping onto a dance floor melts away, and I find myself jumping and twirling next to Raj.

The music pounds like a pulse through the floor, and it's so loud, you can't think. It feels like the undertow of the ocean, and I'm just swept along, everything reduced to senses. The sticky heat of the air. The brush of an elbow. The flash of a strobe light.

I'm a jellyfish glowing in the dark sea, bright and brilliant, just waiting to be discovered.

When the music stops, my eyes meet Raj's and we both gasp, grinning at each other.

And then I look around for my grandfather. He's slumped in a chair on the side of the room, his head nodding into his chest. Fast asleep.

Like an old man.

21
Candles

When I wake up, rainbow-colored helium balloons are bouncing on my ceiling and I'm not eleven anymore. I haven't grown overnight, or changed in any physical way, but I feel different. Everything feels *more*.

My mom walks in, carrying the phone.

"It's your dad," she says, and hands it to me.

"Happy birthday from Houston!" he calls over

the line. "How's it feel to be the wizened old age of twelve?"

"Great!" I say.

"You know what Shakespeare said about growing old?"

"What?"

"When the age is in, the wit is out."

"Oh," I say. "Huh?"

"It's from *Much Ado About Nothing*," he informs me. "He's saying that when you get old, you lose your brains."

"That's good."

"Good?"

"Sure. At least I'll have an excuse when I don't get a perfect report card."

He laughs.

When I open my locker at school, there's a birthday card waiting for me from Brianna. I can't help but remember last year, when she decorated my desk with crepe paper and flowers and brought in a whole box of cupcakes. The card seems a little sad.

But the day gets better.

At lunch, Raj hands me a present with a pink bow.

"Hey," he says. "Happy birthday."

"How'd you know?" I ask.

My grandfather taps his chest. "I told him, of course."

I open the box and grin. It's a burrito from my favorite Mexican place.

"This is great! Thanks!" I tell him.

He blushes a little, looks away.

"When I was a kid, there wasn't this much hoopla around birthdays," my grandfather says from across the table. "You all want a ticker-tape parade. Everything's too much with this generation."

"Uh, you know, *you're* part of this generation now," Raj says.

I've noticed that grown-ups don't seem to get as excited about birthdays as kids do. My mom jokes that she's stopped counting them. Which makes me think.

"How many candles will you have on your cake this year?" I ask my grandfather.

"What?" he asks.

"For your birthday. Because of the *T. melvinus*," I explain. "Will you have seventy-seven candles or, like, fourteen?"

My grandfather blinks and then says, "I don't believe in birthdays."

My mom is a little surprised when I request French food for my birthday dinner.

"French? Not Mexican?" she asks.

"French," I say, and my grandfather gives me an approving look.

The French restaurant where we go to dinner is small and intimate. The napkins are thick and ironed, and the waiter sweeps the crumbs off the table with a fancy little knife.

I order coq au vin and it's delicious. The waiter gives us bowls of sorbet between each course. But the best part of the meal is the end: instead of a dessert cart, the waiter wheels out a cheese cart! There must be twenty kinds of cheese to choose from. Pasteur would be impressed.

Then my mom breaks out the presents from her and my dad. A gift card to a place at the mall that sells hair accessories. A puzzle with a picture of a unicorn (one thousand pieces). And a cell phone! There's even a cute case: pink with glitter.

"Finally!" I say. "Thanks!"

My mom smiles. "Use it wisely." She adds, "Don't go over your minutes."

My grandfather hands me his present. It's a big box wrapped in shiny silver paper with a white bow. I tear the paper away and gasp in delight.

"A microscope!"

"It's a good one, practically professional," my grandfather says.

I stare at the box. It feels like I've been officially ushered into a secret society of scientists.

My grandfather points out the features. "Binocular eyepiece. Halogen light. Four objective lenses. Of course, I'll teach you how to use it."

"Thank you," I tell him, and my throat feels thick. "This is the best present ever!"

"Well, good," he says, a little gruffly. "I'm glad you like it."

My mom watches this byplay with a funny look. "I thought the cell phone would be the best present ever."

After dinner, the waiter brings out a cake. There are thirteen candles—twelve pink ones plus a rainbow candle to grow on. The whole restaurant sings "Happy Birthday" to me.

I lean in and blow out my candles. One refuses to go out and it takes three times before it's finally out.

That night, I fall asleep dreaming of candles. Hundreds of candles. They burn on and on, bright and defiant.

Never going out.

22
Growing Pains

My grandfather walks into the kitchen a few mornings later carrying a bottle of pain pills. He pours a glass of water and pops a handful of pills.

"Are you okay?" I ask him.

He's pale, with dark circles under his eyes. He doesn't look good.

"I'm having growing pains," he grits out,

pointing to his legs. "The *T. melvinus* must be regenerating my bones."

"Does it hurt a lot?" I ask.

"Let's just say I know what it felt like to be tortured on the rack."

My dad's back in town for the weekend. He appears at our front door after lunch, wearing worn-out jeans and a black T-shirt and carrying his toolbox.

"Dad!" I shout, and fling myself at him.

"Reporting for duty," he tells me, holding up his toolbox. "I hear there's a toilet that needs fixing."

My father is handsome. I don't say that just because I'm his daughter. He's the kind of man who women stop and stare at when he walks into a room. He's got thick, curly black hair and dark brown eyes. He's usually cast as the rake or the hero in a play.

"I miss working with my assistant." He winks at me. "I brought your hammer."

To pay the bills when I was little, my dad did carpentry work and odd jobs, hauling me around in my baby carrier. When I started teething, I chewed the wooden handle of one of his hammers. It still has bite marks on it.

"Where's your mother?" he asks.

"At the high school. They're having trouble with the light board," I tell him. "She said you're cooking dinner."

He looks around. "You're here by yourself?"

"No. Melvin's in the den."

"Ah, right," he says. "She mentioned something about some long-lost cousin crashing here. Well, let's get that toilet out of the way."

We settle down in the bathroom, and my father snakes the toilet and then takes the lid off and tinkers around with the insides.

"That should do it," he says. "You want to do the honors?"

I flush and the water goes down.

"You should've been a plumber," I say.

He gives a wry smile. "I would've made a whole lot more money, that's for sure."

My grandfather walks into the bathroom holding

The Catcher in the Rye. He freezes when he sees my father.

"You must be Melvin," my father says. "I'm Ellie's dad, Jeremy." He holds out his hand.

My grandfather doesn't reciprocate. "Did you wash that hand?" he asks.

"Toilet water is clean," my father says.

"Then drink it," my grandfather replies.

We stand there for a minute. Then my grandfather holds up his book.

"You gonna stand around yapping all day?" my grandfather asks. "I have homework to finish."

My father makes risotto for dinner. We sit outside on our tiny patio, and the adults drink red wine and my grandfather and I have soda. Between the crisp air, the good food, and my parents trading gossip about theater friends, it feels like I'm watching a favorite television show. Except this time my grandfather has a guest role as the Silent, Moody Teenager. Or maybe he isn't acting.

My father and grandfather have never exactly been buddies. When my parents first got married, my grandfather said some things to my father that involved the words "punk," "my daughter," and "knocked up." Needless to say, there is no way we can let my dad in on the little secret about Melvin.

My grandfather turns to my dad. "So I hear you're an actor. How's that working out for you?"

"Pretty good, actually," he says. "The tour of my production has been extended for another year."

"That's wonderful, Jeremy!" my mother enthuses.

"Congrats, Dad," I say.

My grandfather doesn't look very impressed. He says, "Lots of money performing in Peoria?"

"I'm in the union," my dad says. "I've got a great benefits package."

My grandfather grunts.

My dad smiles at him, faintly curious. "You remind me of someone," he says.

"Really," my grandfather says. "Who?"

"Just an old guy. One of those grumpy types. Actually, you're distantly related to him. Guess Melvin is a family name."

My mom and I share a worried look.

Then, without a word, my grandfather gets up and goes inside. My father turns to my mother.

"Interesting kid," he says.

"Teenagers," my mom says with a careless roll of her shoulders.

"I'll clear," I offer, and start picking up dishes. My parents beam at me.

I stack the plates, and what I see when I go into the kitchen almost makes me drop them: my grandfather is pouring red wine into a plastic cup.

"What are you doing?" I hiss.

"What does it look like I'm doing?" he says, and drinks from the cup.

"But—but—you can't!"

"Why not?" he grumbles. "It's not like I'm underage. And I need something to dull the pain. My legs are killing me."

The wine loosens my grandfather's tongue, and he starts to make even more snarky remarks at the dinner table.

"To be or not to be thirteen. That is the question," he says.

My parents are deep in conversation and don't seem to notice what's going on. We move inside because it's getting chilly, congregating around the kitchen table.

"I'm going to the bathroom," my grandfather announces, and walks out.

My mother shakes her head and turns to my dad. "Were you like this as a teenage boy?"

"I'm not sure." A puzzled look crosses my dad's face. "Mostly I remember being embarrassed by my parents all the time."

She changes the subject. "So, spill. How's *Francois*?" She makes air quotes with her hands when she says the name.

Francois, I know, is the director of *Les Misérables*.

"You mean besides having a French name but actually being from Long Island?"

"I knew it was a fake accent!" my mom says.

"He had a good speech coach somewhere along the line."

The toilet flushes.

My father adds, "Also, his ego is bigger than a blimp."

The toilet flushes again.

"Did you fix it?" my mom asks him.

"I fixed it," my father insists.

I think of all the pain pills Melvin took earlier. Worry spikes through me.

"Maybe we should check on him," I suggest.

We find my grandfather hunched in front of the toilet, throwing up.

"Oh, no! Do you have food poisoning?" my mom asks when my grandfather turns a gray face to her.

My father sniffs and looks furious.

"Since when does food poisoning smell like red wine?"

23
Pizza Delivery

My grandfather is grounded.

Raj and I wait for him by the flagpole after school. He waits with me most days now. He says the betting money's on my grandfather getting detention again.

My grandfather comes running up to us. He's wild-eyed and frantic.

"I know why they deactivated my key card!

I know why they closed my email account!" he exclaims.

Raj and I look at him.

"The company's been bought! They're moving to Malaysia!"

"Malaysia?" I ask.

"It's all over the Internet! Who knows what's going to happen to my *T. melvinus*? They'll probably just throw it out!"

He slams into the bathroom the minute we get home. I decide to set up my microscope and try to lure him out of his bad mood. It comes with a set of prepared slides. There's a fern spore. A cotton fiber. A salt crystal. And, oddly enough, a goldfish scale. I guess not everybody flushes their fish when they die.

I look at the goldfish scale under the microscope. It's beautiful, a fan of color, and I think of all the Goldies. Maybe they would have lived if they'd had the *T. melvinus* compound. Maybe we'd have a big tank of them swimming around.

The doorbell rings and when I answer it, a kid is standing there holding a pizza box.

"Pizza delivery," he says.

His hair is in a Mohawk, and he's got a few rings in his ears and one in his lip. Delivery boys always look a little sketchy, like they're the kids the malls don't want to hire.

"Hang on," I say, and call my grandfather. "Did you order a pizza?"

"Pepperoni," the kid clarifies.

My grandfather comes to the door. "I didn't order anything," he says with a frown.

"What street number do you have?" I ask the kid. He looks at the slip in his hand and gives an apologetic smile.

"Oops, my mistake," he says, and lopes away.

As I watch him walk away, I remember my grandfather saying how the lab assistants like to eat pizza.

I look at my grandfather and smile.

"I think I know how to get into building twenty-four."

O   O   O

I detail my plan to Raj and my grandfather at the lunch court.

"Raj dresses up as a delivery kid. He takes a real pizza and he gets buzzed in by the lab assistants. He drops it off, and on the way out he grabs the *T. melvinus*. That way, we don't have to worry about the security guard or the whole key-card thing!"

"Not bad," my grandfather says.

I turn to Raj. "What do you think? Would you do it?"

He doesn't hesitate. "Sure. I'm in."

"And your brother, too," my grandfather adds. "We need a ride."

We plan it for Friday; that's the night my mom stays late to run lines with the actors. It should give us plenty of time to get to the lab and back home again without her finding out. It's perfect.

Except that when Raj shows up on our front porch on Friday, he's alone.

"Ananda's car is in the shop," he explains.

We stand around the kitchen trying to figure out what to do.

"He said it should be fixed by next week," Raj tells my grandfather.

My grandfather is frustrated. "I don't want to wait until next week! Who knows what will happen in the meantime to my *T. melvinus*?"

"So let's just take the bus," Raj says.

"Do you know how long it will take if we go by bus? We have to find a pizza place, and then get the pizza, and then take four buses to get there, and walk and . . ."

But I'm not listening to him; I'm too busy staring at my puzzle on the kitchen table. It's almost finished now. The bustle of the city. The people rushing down the sidewalk. The storefronts.

The yellow taxicabs.

24
Nobel

People on television hop in and out of cabs all the time, like it's no big thing. But I've never been in one, and everything about it seems exotic. The meter on the dashboard. The smell of pine air freshener. The way the cabdriver talks nonstop into his headset. He doesn't even seem surprised to have three kids in the back of his cab.

My grandfather has the driver stop at a pizza parlor. He orders two pizzas, four sodas, and breadsticks and gives the kid behind the counter an extra hundred for his cap, his shirt, and a cooler with the pizza-place logo.

It's almost seven when we get to building twenty-four. There are only two cars in the parking lot.

"Looks quiet," I observe.

"Typical Friday night," my grandfather replies in a scathing voice. "Everyone leaves early. This generation has no dedication."

Raj puts on the shirt and cap. He looks perfect. I'm suddenly worried. I touch his arm.

"Don't get caught," I tell him.

He looks at me steadily.

"I won't," he says.

"I'm keeping the meter on," the cabdriver informs us loudly as Raj walks away.

The meter ticks up. Forty dollars. Sixty dollars. Seventy dollars. And then Raj suddenly appears next to the cab, holding the cooler. A wave of relief rushes over me.

"Did you get it?" my grandfather demands.

"Yep," Raj says. "It was a piece of cake. They

didn't even ask me who ordered it. The guy just waved me back."

My grandfather has the cab drop us off at a Chinese restaurant for an impromptu celebration.

"Order anything you want," he tells us. "I'm getting moo goo gai pan."

As if there was any question.

Raj taps on the menu. "They have jellyfish. We should totally order it."

I grin.

The food arrives, and we start eating. Raj bites into the jellyfish.

"What's it taste like?" I ask him.

He chews. And keeps on chewing.

"Rubber bands," he says.

I can't help myself. "Jellyfish: you can use it to organize things!"

He catches my drift right away. "You can use it as an eraser."

"You can bounce it like a Super Ball!"

It's like the crispy corn dog thing, only better.

Raj and I out-jellyfish each other until we're laughing so hard, we can barely breathe.

"So should I wear a bow tie?" my grandfather
asks.

Raj raises an eyebrow. "It's probably a bit much
for middle school."

My grandfather corrects him. "No, to the Nobel
ceremony. It's black-tie."

Raj turns to me. "What should *we* wear?"

"You?" my grandfather scoffs.

"Excuse me. Who got the *T. melvinus* out of the
lab?" he asks.

"He's right," I agree.

My grandfather makes an annoyed noise. "Fine.
But I'm getting primary authorship."

We linger after we're done eating, hogging the
table and reading fortune cookies. The restaurant
is buzzing with the crush of Friday night, but our
table is the center of my universe. I want this night
to last forever.

My grandfather has the waiter bring us more

tea, and he fills our porcelain cups. His college ring is too big on his slender finger.

"A toast," he proposes.

Raj looks at the cooler sitting in a chair. "To jellyfish?"

But I shake my head because I already know the perfect toast.

"To the possible," I say, meeting my grandfather's eyes.

He gives me a small smile.

We all lift our teacups and say, *"To the possible!"*

25
Chill

When I wake up, my bedroom is freezing.

Fall has finally arrived, and my mother doesn't like to turn on the heat unless it's below sixty-five. She says it's California, not Alaska, and I should just put on a sweater.

Even though it's cold, excitement warms my veins.

The *T. melvinus* is safe in the freezer in our garage, and my grandfather is full of plans for what to do next. He wants to get the ball rolling. Rent a space. Set up a real lab. Buy equipment. Refine the compound. Then he'll be able to announce it to the world.

I can hardly sleep waiting for the next part. Is this what Salk felt like when he knew his vaccine had worked? Maybe we *will* win a Nobel Prize.

My grandfather's comments about what to wear tease at me. I've never been to anything fancy. What would I wear? A long dress? High heels? I remember that Marie Curie won a Nobel and wonder what she wore to the awards ceremony. I decide to look it up.

Most pictures show her in old-fashioned black dresses, and her hair was totally frizzy, just like mine. I can't find a photo showing what she wore to accept her Nobel, but I do discover something I hadn't known before. Something my grandfather left out.

Marie Curie was exposed to a lot of radiation during her experiments. Eventually it poisoned her.

Her discovery killed her.

o   o   o

It's windy and chilly on the lunch court. I'm standing in line with my tray, waiting to pay. It's crispy corn dog day.

Across the way, Raj and my grandfather are at our usual table. Their heads are bent together and my grandfather is scribbling in his notebook.

"Hi, Ellie."

I turn around and freeze. It's Brianna.

She's standing behind me, holding a bottle of juice. I wait to feel the burning stab of pain that usually accompanies her appearance, but it doesn't come. There's a twinge, an ache, the way a scraped knee feels after the swelling's gone down. I know I'll be fine.

"Hey," I say. "How's volleyball?"

She hesitates. "It's a lot harder than I thought. Super competitive. I'll have to try out again next season."

"Oh," I say.

There's a moment of awkward silence. Then

Brianna looks down at my tray, gives me one of her old smiles.

"It's a crispy corn dog. I used to love them," she says, and it almost sounds like an apology.

I swallow. "Me too."

And I feel relieved, like this part is over somehow and it's okay. Because I've moved on. I've got my grandfather. And Raj.

"By the way, I saw your old sitter Nicole at the mall," Brianna says. "She said to say hi."

I look across the lunch court at Raj, remember Nicole mentioning her discount. Maybe I could get Raj an earring.

"Who's that boy you're with all the time?" Brianna asks, following my line of sight.

"That's Raj," I say.

"I meant the one with the long hair," she clarifies.

"Oh, that's my cousin Melvin. He's staying with us," I explain.

"I didn't know you had any cousins out here," she says.

"It's kind of a long story."

A dreamy look crosses her face. "He's cute."

I half smile at her. "Huh?"

She bites her lip. "Does he have a girlfriend?"

"Girlfriend?" I echo, and think of my grand-mother's slippers.

"Yeah," she says, and I see the hopeful look in her eyes. "Do you think he'd like me?"

My mind just keeps repeating again and again: *Brianna thinks my seventy-six-year-old grandfather is cute?*

I try to picture them kissing and a cold feeling fills me.

"Ellie?" Brianna says.

I blink.

"What do you think?" she asks. "Would Melvin like me?"

I force myself to respond.

"No," I say firmly. "He's not really interested in that kind of thing."

"Too bad," she says.

26
Mummy

The house is toasty warm when I go into the kitchen to make breakfast. My grandfather is already sitting there, dressed.

My mother stomps in, demanding, "Who turned up the thermostat?"

"Not me," I say.

My grandfather gives her a cool look. "I did."

"Why?"

"Because it's like an ice bucket in this place," he says. "You could preserve dead bodies."

"We're trying to save money," she says.

He digs in his pocket and pulls out a twenty-dollar bill.

"Here," he says. "Turn up the heat."

My mother and Ben are going to see a play a friend of hers is putting on. As they're walking out the front door, my grandfather trails after them.

"What time will you have her home?" he asks Ben.

"Excuse me?" my mom says sarcastically. "I think I'm a little old for a curfew."

"*I'm* the babysitter," my grandfather says. "Don't you think I have a right to know what time you'll be home?"

"I'll have her home by midnight," Ben promises.

I pop popcorn and try to get my grandfather to

watch a monster-movie marathon with me. They're showing a bunch of black-and-white classics—*Creature from the Black Lagoon, The Mummy, Dracula*—but he tells me he's too busy.

"I need to work on my *T. melvinus* paper. I'll have to submit it for peer review," he says.

I'm still watching at midnight when my grandfather walks into the den, looking angry.

"Your mother is late," he says.

Ten minutes later, Ben's car pulls into the driveway and my grandfather races out the front door. I follow him.

He goes right up to Ben's car and bangs on his window. Ben rolls it down and looks at my grandfather in confusion.

"You're ten minutes late!" my grandfather tells him.

"There was an accident," Ben apologizes.

"Then you should have given yourself more time." His voice sounds like a thirteen-year-old's, but it has the authority of an adult's.

After Ben drives away and we go inside, my grandfather and my mother have it out.

"Were you kissing in the driveway? The whole neighborhood could see you!"

My mother throws up her arms. "So what?"

"What kind of example are you setting for your daughter?"

My mom loses it.

"Excuse me, but am I living in 1950? Besides, you're out of line telling *me* what to do."

"I am your father!"

"You may be my father, but *I* am the grown-up around here! You don't tell me what to do!"

"*I'm* the grown-up!" he shouts back at her.

"Have you taken a look at yourself in the mirror lately?" she asks. "Because you are not a grown-up! You're a teenager!"

He glares at her and walks out of the room. We hear the bathroom door slam shut dramatically.

She turns to me.

"See?" she says. "Teenager."

o o o

There's a traveling Egyptian exhibition at the de Young Museum in San Francisco, and Raj invites me to see it with him. My parents love art, and I've practically grown up at the de Young. I know where all the bathrooms are. My dad likes to joke that I potty-trained next to Renaissance masters.

My mom needs to borrow some props from a theater in the city, so she offers to drive us in. I invite my grandfather to come.

"I don't have time to play," he tells me, his fingers flying across the keyboard of his laptop. "I'm working on my patent application."

As we drive through Golden Gate Park, I notice another building, one we must have passed a million times but I've never paid much attention to: the California Academy of Sciences. I suddenly want to know where every bathroom is in it, too.

There's a huge line when we get to the de Young. I had no idea mummies were so popular. Raj fits right in with the San Francisco crowd. Nobody looks at him twice.

We wind our way through the exhibition. In one room, they've re-created the inside of a tomb. The sarcophagus is surrounded by the dead man's belongings: furniture, food, and a pair of leather slippers. It's like his life has been frozen in time, and I can't help but think of my grandfather's apartment.

We finally make our way to the mummy that's the highlight of the exhibition. It's behind glass and is nothing like how I imagined. The body is small—maybe my size—and skinny. The bandages aren't white like in the movies; instead they're a dark brownish black and look like they've been melted onto the body. There's a hole where the nose should be, and the skin looks hard, like suede.

But it's the hair that's the most disturbing. There's a long tuft of brown hair curling on the back of the mummy's head. I almost wish I hadn't seen it; it makes the mummy seem too real.

I don't remember my grandmother's funeral,

but I know she was cremated and her ashes were scattered in San Francisco Bay. There's something I've always liked about that. Whenever I see the bay, I feel like I can hear her in the rolling waves and the shouting seagulls.

"Why did they do all this?" I ask Raj. "Why not just bury the body? Or cremate it?"

"Because they wanted to live forever." He squints a half-smile at me. "They thought their spirit could come back into the body if it was preserved. You know, kind of like what Melvin's doing."

"Melvin's not dead," I say.

"True. But he's sort of preserving himself," he jokes. "Just like a mummy."

I stare at the tuft of hair.

"Hey, come on," Raj says, and smiles. "Let's hit the next room. They've got a mummified cat."

27
After

On the bus ride home from school, my grand-father holds up his science textbook. He must be running low on laundry because he's wearing the cast shirt from my mother's production of *Hair.* It's tie-dyed and I think of Starlily.

"*T. melvinus* will have its own chapter in here now!" he crows.

"Yeah," I say with a forced smile.

He starts paging through the sections. "Hmm, where would it make most sense for them to put it?"

When we get home, my grandfather heads to the kitchen for a snack, but I'm not hungry. My stomach feels a little weird, so I go into my bedroom and lie down. I can't stop thinking about mummies. It's so creepy. The dead waiting to come back to life. Maybe there's a reason they're monsters in horror movies.

I look around my room with new eyes, and what I observe makes me question everything. The handprints on the wall: as people grow older, will hands get smaller instead of bigger because of *T. melvinus*? The pink bow on my dresser, from the birthday present Raj gave me: will people have fewer candles on their cake every year because they're getting younger? I feel like Galileo, my vision of the universe suddenly upended.

Before I know it, I find myself sitting at the computer, looking up the atomic bomb and Oppenheimer. All at once, I need to know about the *after*.

What happened *after* the bombs were dropped on Japan?

Images flash across the screen. Crushed buildings. Smoke. Crying children.

The article says that no one knows for sure how many people died from the bombings. One estimate puts the final death toll at 185,000. I'm good at math. I try to make this number something I can actually understand. There are nine hundred kids at our middle school, so it would be two hundred middle schools' worth of dead kids.

Of kids like Raj. And Momo. And Brianna.

And that's not even counting everyone else—like the school secretary and the janitor and all the teachers. Mr. Ham, with his funny ties.

My head swims.

What if it happens again? Like Mr. Ham said: the genie is out of the bottle. Oppenheimer's words ring in my ears like a thousand bombs going off at once.

We knew the world would not be the same.

O   O   O

My grandfather's at the kitchen counter with his laptop, eating a burrito and drinking tea.

The words bubble up out of me.

"What will they write?" I ask him.

"About what?"

"About us. In the textbooks. What will they write?"

He stares at me.

"I mean, will they say that Melvin Sagarsky and Ellie Cruz changed the world? Or that we ruined it?"

"Ruined? We're saving people from old age! Just like polio."

"But old age isn't the same as polio," I say.

He shakes his head. "What has gotten into you? This is science! This is how discovery works!"

"I believe in science! But what if it isn't a good idea? What if we're not Salk? What if we're Oppenheimer? What if *T. melvinus* is like the bomb?"

"Nonsense," he says, and turns back to his computer, dismissing me.

"Brianna thinks you're cute!" I burst out.

He turns to me with a perplexed look. "Who's Brianna?"

"My friend! Ex-friend. I don't even know who she is anymore, but it doesn't matter. She wants to date you!"

"I'm a widower. I have no interest in dating."

He doesn't get it. He's like Marie Curie with the radiation. He doesn't see that it's going to poison everything.

"You're—you're like a mummy! Coming back to life!"

"You're not making any sense at all," he says to me, like he's speaking to a toddler who's having a tantrum.

I stare at his tie-dyed shirt, and I suddenly understand what Starlily was trying to teach us with the goldfish. Endings are sad. Like goldfish dying and Grandma's slippers and Brianna and me. But beginnings are exciting. Like discovering something I might be good at and making new friends. Raj.

"It's the cycle of life," I say, remembering

Starlily's words. "Things need to move forward, not backward."

"Who wants to move forward? Not me."

My mind is racing now and I think of things not moving forward. Like my mom. She's scared of making a mistake again, even though anyone can see that Ben's the perfect missing piece for her puzzle.

"What about the whole law-of-motion thing? You're supposed to keep moving or you get stuck! Like Mom with Ben!"

"She can do better than him," my grandfather says, ignoring what I'm really saying.

"What if we've gone too far? What if we ruin the whole world?"

"So dramatic," he observes. "Just like your mother."

"What about the trash cans?" I ask.

"I'll put them out tonight," he says.

"How's that going to work? When all the old people are young again, who's going to be in charge? Who's going to decide when to put out the trash cans and turn up the heat? *Who's going to be the grown-up?"*

He looks momentarily off balance, as if he hasn't considered this. Then his expression hardens.

"You don't understand. You haven't had to live through this," he says.

The words tumble from my mouth before I can stop them. "But I want to!"

I look at him imploringly. "Is growing up, growing old—*life*—is it all so terrible?"

His eyes go still, and he looks at me, like he's seeing me for the first time.

I take a deep breath, remember the feeling of dancing on that dark floor, the music pounding through me, the possibility of *something*—I don't know what—so close, and I want to feel that again.

"Because I want to try it," I whisper. "I'm only twelve."

The garage door rumbles open. My mom walks into the kitchen carrying bags of takeout.

"I picked up Chinese," she says with a smile.

"And, yes, Dad, I got you moo goo gai pan and extra soy sauce."

He stares at the bags and then at me.

"I'm not hungry," he says, and walks out.

My mom turns to me. "Guess there's a first time for everything."

28
Observation

I'm wearing my warmest sweater, but it does nothing to warm the chill between me and my grandfather.

At the lunch court, he eats his lunch in two bites and then races off.

"What's going on with you guys?" Raj asks me.

"We had a fight," I say.

"About what?"

"Just stuff," I hedge.

As if "stuff" can describe a disagreement about the fate of all humankind.

My mom hates having a half-empty theater on opening night, so she enlists me to help fill the unsold seats for *Our Town*. She gives me a ton of free tickets to pass out around school.

During science class, I ask Momo if she'd like some.

"They're free," I explain. "My mom's the director."

"Sure," she says. "Will you be going?"

I make a face. "Oh, I'll be there."

She laughs. "I know the feeling. I have to go to all my brother's soccer games." Then she says, "You want to do something after? Maybe get some frozen yogurt?"

I smile at her. "That sounds great!"

Our Town opens on Friday night. My mom's already at the theater getting everything ready, so Ben drives my grandfather and me over. My grand-father's wearing a jacket and tie. I expect him to complain about having to see *Our Town*, but he's unusually quiet.

The theater is packed. I guess all my hard work paid off. I wave at Momo, who looks like she brought her whole family. We settle down in our seats. The houselights go dark and the curtain comes up.

Maybe I was too young when I saw it all those times before, because this time it's interesting. Or maybe it's the actors. My mom was right—the kids playing Emily and George are great, especially Emily.

She starts out as a teenager. She grows up, gets married, and then dies while having her second baby. After she's dead, she comes back to Earth for one day—as a twelve-year-old. Just like me.

She has a line about whether anyone under-stands life when they're living it. I get what she's trying to say: life is precious and we don't real-ize that at the time. But maybe life's also precious because it doesn't last forever. Like an amusement park ride. The roller coaster is exciting the first time. But would it be as fun if you did it again and again and again?

I can't help myself; I glance at my grandfather. His eyes are locked on the stage, transfixed. As if sensing me looking at him, he glances at me. Our eyes meet and hold. Something in his face softens, and I think for a moment that he gets it, too. That he *understands*.

But then he blinks.

And looks away.

The play gets great reviews. They even get a standing ovation on closing night. But at home, there's no clapping, no encore. It's just me and my grandfather not talking to each other.

I put a new packet of ponytail holders out for him in the bathroom as a sort of peace offering, but he just leaves them there.

Part of me wants to smooth everything over, tell

him I was wrong. But deep down, I know I'm right. The world isn't ready for *T. melvinus.* I wonder if this is what it's like to be a scientist. To believe in something so strongly that you're willing to go against everything, even someone you love.

Maybe I am a little bit mad after all.

The house is empty when we get home from school. My mom's at the high school striking the set. My grandfather and I go our separate ways: me to the kitchen, him to the bathroom.

I'm full of nervous energy and decide to cook something. I flip through my grandmother's recipe box and settle on quiche. I make sure we have all the ingredients: flour and butter for the crust, eggs, ham, cheese. There's only one block of cheese, and it's way in the back of the refrigerator. When I pull it out, I realize it must have been in there for a long time: there's fuzzy blue-green mold growing on it. My first reaction is to be grossed out, but my second reaction is to be intrigued. I kind of want to see what it looks like under a microscope.

I get my microscope and set it up at the kitchen counter. I scrape off some of the mold, put it on a slide, and look at it through the eyepiece. It looks like delicate threads.

My grandfather walks into the kitchen, carrying *The Catcher in the Rye*.

"The toilet's clogged again," he tells me. "What are you looking at?"

I feel awkward explaining it to him. "I was making a quiche, but the cheese was all moldy, so I decided to observe the mold under the microscope."

He gives me an unfathomable look and says, "Of course you did. That's what a scientist would do."

I don't know what to say.

My grandfather holds up the book. "I finished it. It was good."

My mouth drops open. "It was?"

"Yes. I judged it prematurely and I was wrong about it." He hesitates. "About other things, too."

He plucks an apple from the bowl of fruit. It's red and bruised, almost starting to go.

"You were right," he says with a lift of his shoulders.

I hold my breath, waiting. Hoping.

He looks at the apple. "The seed is planted, it grows into a tree, the fruit ripens, falls onto the ground." He takes a bite. Juice drips down his chin. "And then it starts all over again. The cycle of life. I don't need to be Galileo to make that observation."

I swallow.

"Science is powerful. There are always consequences—wonderful and terrible. I suppose I lost my way for a moment in all the excitement and forgot what Salk said."

"What did he say?"

His eyes meet mine. "Our greatest responsibility is to be good ancestors."

I nod.

Then he heaves a great sigh. "I guess this means I won't be getting a Nobel."

"Scientists don't give up. You can still get a Nobel someday. For something even more important. Something that nobody's ever done before!"

"And what would that be?" he asks, sounding skeptical.

I point to the pimple on my chin. "Finding a cure for acne."

"Hmm. That *would* be revolutionary." He shakes his head. "Enough about all this. Is the plunger in the garage? I need to use it to clear the toilet. It took a few tries to get the *T. melvinus* down."

"You flushed it? Why didn't you just put it in the trash?"

He scoffs. "The trash? Your mother would probably forget to put it out. Then raccoons would get into the cans and eat the *T. melvinus*, and who knows what would happen next? Vicious raccoons that never get old rampaging around the neighborhood?"

We laugh.

29
Happy Beginnings

Nicole calls to tell my mom that she wants her old babysitting job back. The ear-piercing place is not turning out to be the great opportunity she thought it would be. My grandfather greets this news with enthusiasm.

"It's time for me to move on anyway," he informs us.

I look at him in horror. "You're leaving?"

"I'll be back. Don't worry about that," he says.

"I have to make sure you get into a decent PhD program."

"But who's going to look after you?" my mother exclaims. "You're thirteen years old!"

My grandfather gives my mother a steady look. "Melissa, we both know this isn't working out. There are things I want to do—that I need to do. And I'll look after myself. I'm a grown-up."

She looks like she wants to disagree, but then she purses her lips.

"Where will you go?" I ask him.

"I'm not sure exactly. I thought I'd travel. Take a bus ride." He pauses. "See the country."

I remember my grandmother's dream.

My mother arranges for movers to put everything from his apartment in storage. She also gets him a cell phone and puts him on our family plan so that he can stay in touch on the road.

On the day he's leaving, we wait with him in the bus station. It's bustling with people coming and going, rushing to catch buses leaving for everywhere. My grandfather's not sure where he's going. He says he has nothing but time and money.

"Will you be okay?" my mother asks him.

"Of course I will. I have two PhDs," he says firmly.

I hand him my going-away present.

"What's this?" he asks, surprised.

He opens the wrapped box and looks at what's inside: my collection of ponytail holders.

Tears prick at my eyes. I don't want him to leave. I grab him, hug him tight.

"I love you," I say.

My grandfather hugs me back, whispers in my ear, "I believe in you, Ellie. You're my *possible*."

I watch him board the bus and know I will never look at a bowl of fruit or cheese, or anything ever, in the same way again. It turned out that what I needed to teach me about life was my grandfather.

He was the fourteenth goldfish.

O   O   O

Everything's back to the way it was before, but it doesn't feel the same. The house is oddly empty. Who knew you could miss the smell of teenage-boy socks?

I decide my room needs a makeover; I don't want to look at all those little handprints anymore. My dad helps me one weekend when he's home. We paint the walls a deep sea blue. We use glow-in-the-dark paint to add jellyfish near the ceiling. When I lie in bed at night, it feels like I'm on the bottom of the ocean.

Ananda has started his college search. Raj and I go with him the day he checks out Berkeley. The campus is beautiful, the lawns green and bustling with students. I can almost see Oppenheimer striding around, full of purpose.

Momo and I have been spending a lot of time together lately. She's into scary films, too. We discover a whole category of old horror films about science gone wrong (*Frankenstein, The Invisible Man, Tarantula, Godzilla, The Fly*). Our favorite is *Them!* It's about a bunch of ants that turn into giant ant-monsters after being exposed to radiation during the New Mexico atomic bomb tests. We even convince Mr. Ham to do a class about monster movies and science. It's fun hanging out with another girl again.

And there are other new beginnings. When Ben comes over to take my mother out to dinner, she meets him at the door, dressed and ready to go, waiting like a teenager on her first date.

She steps across the threshold and into his arms, startling him.

"Yes," she says.

He looks confused, but I know what she's saying.

"I'll marry you."

They have a small ceremony at City Hall, with me as their witness. Ben wears a blue tie to match my mother's hair.

"I love happy endings," the judge tells the newlyweds.

"It's not a happy ending," I correct her.

She looks at me quizzically.

"It's a *happy beginning.*"

o   o   o

I pay twenty dollars to join the Official Melvin Sagarsky Fan Club. I'm the 232nd member. They mail me a welcoming kit from Helsinki, Finland. It includes a membership card and a T-shirt with a picture of my grandfather on the front. He's staring at the camera, a Melvin-esque expression on his face.

I miss him.

And then the slippers start arriving. Bunny slippers. Fuzzy pink slippers. Thickly lined bootie slippers. Leopard-print slippers. Zebra slippers.

The latest package contains slippers that look like alligators and a postcard from St. Augustine, Florida. There's a picture of an archway that says FOUNTAIN OF YOUTH. On the back, my grandfather has included a mailing address and has written:

HA!

P.S. My fan club has invited me to speak at their annual conference in Helsinki!

I send him a care package with hair bands and another book by the author of *The Catcher in the Rye*. It's called *Franny and Zooey*.

I'm working on a new puzzle at the kitchen table when Nicole walks in. It's Egyptian-themed, with a picture of the pyramids and King Tut's sarcophagus. Raj got it for me.

"Your mom called," Nicole tells me. "She and Ben are going to be late. She said we could order a pizza."

My mother and Ben are meeting with a real estate agent about looking for a new house. Something bigger, with a toilet that doesn't get clogged and a yard so I can get a dog.

We call for a pizza, and the doorbell rings five minutes later.

"That was fast," I say.

When I answer the door, there's no pizza-delivery

kid. Instead, a courier van is pulling away from the curb.

"Looks like you got a package," Nicole says.

There's a box on the front porch. The label says CONTAINS DRY ICE.

"What is it?" she asks.

I look at the label. It's addressed to my grandfather and is from somewhere in the Philippines. There's an envelope taped to the package, and I open it. Inside is a handwritten note, and when I read it, my breath stops. It says:

> Dear Dr. Sagarsky,
>   I found a jellyfish even stranger than the last one. Thought you might want it.
>   —Billy

The ~~End~~ Beginning

Author's Note

I have always been inspired by science. As with Ellie, my connection was sparked by someone very close to me: my father.

My father, William Wendell Holm, MD, was involved in two wars in which scientists played a significant role: World War II and the War on Polio. He served in the navy during World War II, and later he became a pediatrician and vaccinated children against polio. When I was growing up, he kept petri dishes with blood agar in our refrigerator to grow bacteria cultures. They were usually on the same shelf as the cottage cheese.

All the scientists mentioned in this book were real people. The discoveries of Galileo Galilei, Isaac Newton, Louis Pasteur, Marie Curie, Robert Oppenheimer, and Jonas Salk changed the world in ways that still echo today.

You, too, can be a scientist. Observe the world

around you. Ask questions. Talk to your teachers. Don't give up.

Be inspired by the scientists who came before you, and fall in love with discovery.

Most of all, believe in the possible.

Acknowledgments

With thanks to Robert J. Malone, executive director of the History of Science Society

Recommended Resources for Continuing the Conversation

Marie Curie and the Nobel Prize
nobelprize.org/nobel_prizes/themes/physics/curie
/index.html
History of Science
hssonline.org
Manhattan Project
amnh.org/exhibitions/past-exhibitions/einstein
/peace-and-war/the-manhattan-project
Isaac Newton
newtonproject.sussex.ac.uk/prism.php?id=1
Louis Pasteur
accessexcellence.org/RC/AB/BC/Louis_Pasteur.php
Jonas Salk
salk.edu/about/jonas_salk.html
Scientists
Fortey, Jacqueline. *DK Eyewitness: Great Scientists.*
London: DK Publishing, 2007.

JENNIFER L. HOLM grew up in a medical family. Her father was a pediatrician and her mother was a pediatric nurse. It wasn't unusual for Jenni to open the kitchen refrigerator and find petri dishes of blood agar that her father was using to culture bacteria. She grew up listening to him talk about the wonder of antibiotics and Jonas Salk and how science could change the world.

Today, Jennifer is the *New York Times* bestselling author of three Newbery Honor Books, as well as the cocreator of the popular Babymouse series (an Eisner Award winner) and Squish series, which she collaborates on with her brother Matthew Holm. You can find out more about her by visiting jenniferholm.com.